Something was _____ _____ _____ e. I could feel it pres_____ _____, but it was there, somehow _____ _____ head.

Panic shot thr_____ _____. And a kind of horrible despair, too. This spirit, or monster, or whatever I'd brought back with me, was in control all the time now. Even by day, this wasn't my bedroom any more.

Now I could feel it pressing down even harder. I started shivering. This was like those nightmares when you know something bad is reaching out for you but you can't move. I shot to my feet.

'We've got to get out of here,' I gasped.

PETE JOHNSON

THE DEAD HOUR

MAMMOTH

First published in Great Britain 1993
by Mammoth
an imprint of Reed International Books Ltd
Michelin House, 81 Fulham Road, London SW3 6RB
and Auckland, Melbourne, Singapore and Toronto

Reprinted 1994 (twice), 1995, 1996

ISBN 0 7497 1460 3

A CIP catalogue record for this title
is available from the British Library

Printed and bound in Great Britain
by Cox & Wyman Ltd, Reading, Berkshire

Contents

Dedicated to

Janetta, Linda and Robin,
Darren Rumble, Bill Bloomfield, Rose Jewitt
and Martin Heffron.

With deep appreciation and affection.

BY RICHARD

When it's dark and I'm in the house on my own, I'm scared of just about everything.

But then everything changes at night, doesn't it? Like my bedroom. By day my bedroom is my good friend. But in the dark it is another place entirely. Suddenly, nothing is familiar any more. I can't even see my room's boundaries.

I reach out for my hi-fi. It isn't there. Why should it be? This isn't my bedroom. This is a strange, disturbing recreation of my bedroom.

Perhaps that's why things you can never imagine in the day come to you at night. The darkness becomes a blank canvas on which you conjure up terrible thoughts and ideas.

I lie here, thinking about ghosts and poltergeists and what it would be like to be buried alive. And once I start thinking about these things I can't stop. No wonder I even think I hear strange sounds in my room.

And it's so shaming, because I'm a seventeen-year-old guy, doing 'A' Levels. I've just passed my driving test and I drive a white Metro for goodness sake. I should have left these fears behind years ago. And in the day, I have. Yet, at night . . . at night . . . but I'm just too old to be scared of the dark. I've got to confront my fears, fight back with reason, logic. Instead of lying here thinking about the supernatural, I should be investigating it. I should find out if ghosts really do exist. I need some proof, some answers.

That's why Danny and myself decided to visit the most haunted place we knew; an old deserted church on Abbotts Hill. There were that many tales about the place it must have wall to wall ghosts. So we would go on a ghost hunt there. If we see something, well, at least I'd know there is another world, a world which seems to be reaching out for me.

But much more likely, we won't see anything. And all I have to fear is my imagination. That is my only enemy.

CHAPTER 1

THE GHOST HUNT

Soon the ghost hunt gained two more people: Angie, Danny's very steady girlfriend, and Louise, a friend of Angie's, who apparently 'liked me'. She'd never spoken to me, just seen me drifting around college in my usual haze, but that was enough: she 'liked me'.

Not that I totally trusted Angie. Have you noticed how people who are in couples are always trying to push you into getting serious with someone too? Incidentally, when Danny first went out with Angie, I had a girlfriend too. I went a bit over the top about her, actually. And I made one fatal mistake: I trusted her completely.

Then one night I turned up unexpectedly down the pub, and I saw her with this geek. She didn't see me. She was too busy taking half his neck off. I thought at least she could have done it somewhere private. It was totally humiliating. But still I didn't want to finish with her. Don't ask me why.

So when she came round I was all set to 'forgive her'. Only then it turned out she'd been seeing the geek for weeks. She said that it had been over between us for some time but she hadn't known how to tell me.

I don't think I really understand relationships. That's why I haven't gone out with anyone since. Anyway, we were waiting for Angie and Louise and they were late (Angie is always late). I was getting worked up, both about Abbotts Hill and, to my annoyance, about this mystery girl who liked me.

So then Danny was asking me about Abbotts Hill. Danny and I have been friends for years. In fact, we are a team, Danny and me. He is the front man; loud, fat, amusing, while I sit back a bit watching people, picking up all the clues. Tonight though, I sussed that Danny was nervous about this expedition. Then I started winding Danny up and the more heated he got, the more relaxed I felt.

What really unnerved Danny was when I said, 'The only thing you've got to watch out for about Abbotts Hill is if the darkness seems to move, for then you will have glimpsed the terrible, dark spirit.'

'What are you going on about?' asked Danny. But I could tell I had him hooked.

'This spirit is a huge, dark figure, which people only see for a second, but if you do see him, you never forget his glowing purple eyes. And you know that you have seen the thing that men fear most: a spirit of death. For his presence means that you, or someone close to you, is going to die, very soon.' My imagination was racing now, as I went on, 'You cannot escape from the spirit either. Once you have seen it, you will go on seeing it until . . .'

I paused dramatically. 'And you cannot keep the spirit out of your house.'

'It comes gliding through the air-conditioning, does it?' said Danny, mockingly. But his eyes were wide with fear.

'You laugh but the dark spirit will break apart the world you know; your world will crumble, disappear. And however fast you run, whenever you look round, it will be there . . . That's what they say, anyway,' I added airily.

Danny stared at me. 'I don't know why we're going there. You said we were just going to see if there were any ghosts up there, but this dark spirit thing . . . it's not worth the risk.'

'I think it is,' I said. 'I mean, we'll know if the dark spirit really exists.'

'Yeah, when we're dead. No, that's it. I'm ringing Angie, we're not going up there.' Then he looked at me and saw me smiling. 'Wind-up merchant,' he called and thumped me on the shoulder. 'I didn't think you'd have the guts to go up there if there really was this dark spirit . . . So you just made all this up?'

I nodded.

'I'd hate to have your imagination,' he said.

Then the doorbell rang, making us both jump. Angie bustled in: smallish, smiley, with mousey-blonde hair that had a white streak down the middle. You'd think it had been bleached in, but actually it was natural; her mum has got the same. Danny calls it her vampire streak and he's the only person who can get away with that.

Angie said, 'Louise, meet Danny and Rich, the two hunkiest guys I know, not.'

Then Louise appeared. I didn't recognise her at all, but then I walk around in a dream. She was quite small with dark bobbed hair, high eyebrows which came up into a big arch, very full lips and shiny green eyes. She was dressed quite plainly (unlike Angie) in black jersey, jeans and boots. Yet, she looked most attractive. I decided she was one of those girls who could wear a sack and still look good.

She smiled nervously at me. 'I don't know how Angie talked me into this.'

'Don't worry,' I said, mock-bravely. 'We'll protect you.'

'Oh, you've really reassured Louise now,' said Angie. 'And if you hate tonight, Rich is to blame. This ghost-hunting was all his idea.'

'I've heard some pretty strange stories about Abbotts Hill,' said Louise.

'Most of them made up by Rich,' murmured Danny.

Louise smiled at me. 'Aren't you frightened by Abbotts Hill?'

I smiled back. 'Nothing scares me,' I said.

CHAPTER 2

THE SPIRIT OF DEATH

As we sped along to Abbotts Hill we started telling ghost stories. Some of the stories sent chills down my spine. Yet, they were oddly cosy, too. In the car, ghosts seemed as unreal as Dracula or Frankenstein. The only story I can remember now was the one Louise told.

She said in a low, quiet tone, 'This is a story about Abbotts Hill from years and years ago. It's all about these children. They lived near Abbotts Hill but they were told by their parents never to play around there because, even then, it had a bad reputation. Of course, that only made the children want to play there all the more. So one day four of them sneaked off to Abbotts Hill and they ran all around the old, deserted church and they decided to play hide and seek in the graveyard. So this little girl found an empty coffin. She climbed in, but the lid fell on top of her.

'The other children ran all around the graveyard trying to find her, but in the end, they decided she must have gone home to tea and went off for their tea as well. Then, when they found out the little girl was missing, they were too scared to tell their parents where they had been. Days went by and there was still no sign of the little girl. Then, finally, the children confessed to their parents that they had gone to Abbotts Hill. There was a search party and at last, they opened the coffin and found her little corpse. It wasn't a pleasant sight. And inside the coffin were all these scratch marks . . .' Louise stopped and for a second caught my eye. I felt she wanted to see my reaction. But, to be honest, I didn't know how to react.

'What a terrible story,' said Angie. 'Is it true?'

Louise nodded.

'Poor little girl,' said Angie. 'What a horrible death.'

'Death is usually horrible,' said Louise, in the same quiet voice she'd told the story. Yet I sensed she was genuinely upset by what she'd told us. That's why I had to say, 'Anyway, she won that game, didn't she?'

Danny laughed while Angie said, 'Oh, that's sick.'

I went on, 'And can't you push a coffin lid up? It doesn't lock like a freezer, does it? And I don't believe she would have found an empty coffin like that.'

'You have to spoil it, don't you, Richard?' said Angie, in that bantering tone she often adopts with me. 'I believe you anyway, Louise.'

'It's just a story,' Louise said, dreamily.

'And it's a great story, make a really good film,' I said, eager not to appear as if I were putting Louise down. 'It's just not true.'

'And Richard knows about these things,' said Angie. 'Eeer, can anyone else smell Danny's trainers?'

'There is a subtle hint of Reebok in the car,' I said.

'They reek,' declared Angie.

'That's because they're getting excited,' said Danny, who was poring over the map, 'because we're almost there, I think. Take it slow here, Rich, if you take a right . . . Actually I think we've just gone past it. Yes, we have.'

'Oh, well done, Danny,' said Angie.

'It's okay,' I said, 'we can turn round up here. That's not a police car behind me, is it, Danny?'

'No, mate, you're all right,' signalled Danny.

I explained, 'The villagers hate people going up to Abbotts Hill at night and they call the police if they see anyone suspicious. On Halloween, the police seal the whole place off.' I turned the car round, then announced, 'Now everyone, keep your eyes peeled.'

'There,' cried Danny and Angie together.

I turned right up this narrow dirt track. I had the headlights on full beam now as my car bumped its way up. There were bushes on either side of the track which flopped right over. It felt as if they were grabbing out at us, trying to stop us reaching the top.

'It's a long way up, isn't it?' mumbled Louise.

'So there's no way we can rush back down again,' I replied.

'Wouldn't it be awful if we ran out of petrol now,' quipped Angie.

'Yeah, there are no garages up here,' I muttered. 'Or if there are, they'll be run by a druid or something.'

The dirt track finally ended and we jolted to a stop. It was so dark I couldn't see anything at first. This is it, I thought and I really felt as if I was about to cross over into . . . what? I wasn't exactly sure. This universe is but a shadow. Where had I heard that? I couldn't remember. But the sentence kept jumping about in my head.

For a moment we all sat in the car staring at each other. Louise gave me a small smile, which was oddly appealing. She seemed both sophisticated and girlish at the same time.

'Okay, now we've seen it, shall we go?' said Danny.

'We've got to get out,' I said. We couldn't bottle out now.

'Yes,' said Louise. 'Come on everyone.'

'Well I'm staying in the middle,' said Danny.

We got out of the car. At first I couldn't see anything at all. Then I made out some roots sticking up out of the ground. I could hear rustling too. My eyes swung upwards and I sighted the outline of a large tree. I moved closer and then a white gate revealed itself. I led the expedition through the gate and out on to a large field.

'So where's the church?' asked Angie. And it was exactly then that the church seemed to jump out at us. All at once it was so close it caught my breath. It had been there all the time, of course, its blank windows alert, watchful, waiting.

There was nothing now to suggest it had ever

been a church. It had no roof, its tower was broken in half and there were whopping great gaps where the stained glass windows must have been. It was crumbling away and looked as if it was about ready to be demolished. It wasn't even that big. It was just a burnt-out shell of a place. Yet somehow, it loomed over us. It didn't want us to go any further, because it had its secrets.

Suddenly Danny grabbed my arm. At first I thought he was messing about, then he pointed ahead of him.

'Look.'

I followed his gaze, taking in the hedges which surrounded the fields. And it was then I noticed the gravestones were all in a circle, stretching right around the church. But Danny was pointing at something beyond the gravestones. 'Down there, I saw something move.'

'I can't see anything,' I said.

'Well I did. I swear on your life I did,' said Danny. 'Cheers everyone and see you back at the car.'

'Danny, there's nothing,' I began, but then, just for a second, I saw something too. A flicker of red light from behind the graves. I turned to Louise and Angie and realised they had seen it too. Now, we couldn't have stood any closer together.

'What is it?' whispered Louise.

'I don't know,' I whispered back. Was this a genuine glimpse of the other world? I felt suddenly excited. For this meant I might not just be spooking myself up at night. Maybe there were things out there which I was picking up. I stared in wonderment after the light. And then I saw it again. Only this time, with a horrible thud of certainty, I knew what it was: a man-made light, probably a camping light.

'It's just a human,' I said slowly. 'Someone's camping down by the gravestones.'

'As you do,' murmured Angie.

'It's probably some nutter with a baseball bat,' said Danny. 'He's bound to be tooled up. And are we staying to find out?'

At once Angie and Danny were racing towards the car.

But I found myself turning towards the old church again, where something caught the corner of my eye. Something which appeared much blacker than the sky above it. And then there was what seemed like a flash of movement.

I didn't run. I couldn't move, just stood there paralysed with fear. I'd just seen something move, a black shape.

The dark spirit. The Spirit of Death.

But that was nonsense. I'd just made that up. I stared again at the church. It was as still as before. What I'd seen was only the darkness shifting. Darkness does that. I know from my bedroom at night.

And then I felt a touch on my shoulder. I whirled around and there was Louise staring at me. Only her eyes were suddenly huge with fear. For a moment I thought she'd seen the black shape too. But then she said, 'Are you all right? Everyone else has gone to the car.'

'I thought I saw . . .' I began. But then I noticed she was shaking. I reached out to her. She grabbed my hand.

'This place is rigged to scare, isn't it?' she said.

I nodded. I thought again of the shape I'd seen moving. That was nothing but my imagination, of course. No point in telling Louise about it.

'Let's go, shall we?' I said, still holding on to her hand. We sped over to Danny and Angie, who were waiting impatiently by the car.

Somehow, going down the hill took longer than going up. It was like travelling down a massive tunnel: the trees were like black walls, blocking out any sense of space. Strange thoughts grew in my mind. I even started wondering if we'd come out in another time and see horses and carts going round.

I was so relieved when we finally hit the road again. Now we were all talking.

'So why was that guy camping up there?' asked Angie.

I'd almost forgotten about him.

'Because he's mad. Like us,' said Danny. 'Anything could have happened up there and we couldn't have defended ourselves. We didn't even have a torch between us . . .'

'That is not a happy place,' said Angie.

'I don't know,' I said. 'In the day I bet that place'd be nothing at all. No, we went up there to be scared and we were.' I wanted to add, 'I even thought I saw a dark shape, just like the one I'd made up for Danny – only it didn't have purple eyes.' I wanted to say those words so much and for everyone to laugh loudly at my over-active imagination. But somehow, the words wouldn't form in my mouth.

Instead, Angie was saying, 'Come on, you were pretty jumpy up there.'

'Not me, Angie,' I said in a gruff voice.

'My next-door neighbour, Harry, the medium, told me not to go up there,' said Danny. 'He said there were bad vibes.'

I laughed loudly. 'Your neighbour Harry knows as much about spirits as my left nostril.'

'No, Harry's a good old boy,' said Danny.

I waved a dismissive hand. 'He's just a big con, like Abbotts Hill.' I turned to Louise. 'You're very quiet.'

She looked up at me. 'Just thinking about it all,' she said. 'I wanted to see if . . .' she stopped and half-laughed. And she hardly said anything else all the way home. We reached her house first. Danny and Angie exchanged knowing smiles when I got out and saw her to the door.

'Thanks for letting me come along today,' she said. She gave me one of her small, sincere smiles. 'I guess we were both hoping to see something tonight.'

She looked directly at me. She had a habit of doing that, I noticed, as if she were collecting something you'd said to be thought about again later. It was flattering, intriguing. Then to my surprise she leaned forward and said, 'I've seen you round the college, you know, in your big coat, looking like someone out of a Clint Eastwood western. And you always seemed to be frowning.' She said this so affectionately, I felt she was paying me a huge compliment.

'I wish I'd seen you before,' I said. 'Still, now I know you . . .' I hovered awkwardly. 'I might give you a ring sometime.'

'742680,' she replied promptly, before smiling again and disappearing into her house.

I stared after her. Then I thought to myself, be careful now. Don't get too hooked.

I dropped Danny and Angie off, then I drove home. To my surprise, the light was on in the kitchen. My mum and dad usually went to bed annoyingly early. My first thought was Nan. There was a time when I saw Nan all the time. But lately she'd been very ill and the idea of seeing her all frail and doddery scared me. I'd rather wait until she was herself again. Or that's what I told myself. The trouble was, the Nan I knew, the Nan I loved, never seemed to be coming back.

I rushed inside. Mum and Dad were sitting round the table with mugs of tea.

'Is anything wrong?' I asked.

'Nan's had a bit of a turn,' said Mum.

'She's always having turns now,' I said. I couldn't help sounding indignant, as if Nan were letting me down with all this illness.

'But she's better now,' said Mum. Then she added, 'Don't forget it's her birthday next week. I know she'd love to see you – and you are on half term.'

'Yes, yes, I'll see her,' I said. I hated the way Mum felt she had to push me to see Nan. I was very close to Nan, closer than to my own parents, in fact. For although my nan liked to tell her stories (which I enjoyed anyhow) you could always talk to her about what was happening now. Actually, my nan used to be pretty amazing. And she would be again.

I went upstairs and crawled into bed. I lay thinking about Nan and, to my surprise, Louise, then fell asleep. I don't know how long I slept. I just remember waking up with a terrible shudder. I always hated waking up at this time. For this was when the darkness was at its thickest, swallowing everything around it: tables, chairs, people.

If only darkness would stay outside the house, like the weather. But instead, it had crept right across my room, wiping out everything I knew and leaving me stranded, alone.

I realised again just how weak I was. No wonder more people die in the middle of the night than at any other time. This is when I'll die too. The dead hour. The time when the Spirit of Death rules, ruthlessly gathering up all those who are too tired and ill to fight any more. Like my nan. No, my nan was a fighter. She'd never submit to the Spirit of Death.

The Spirit of Death. I laughed to myself. I created him to scare Danny and I ended up just scaring myself as usual. I do that so well. Just like now, I've started imagining this tiny, rustling sound. I really think I can hear something out there.

NO, STOP. WHY AM I SCARING MYSELF LIKE THIS?

I rolled on to my side. All I wanted was to go to sleep. I must shut down my imagination now. I

22

closed my eyes tightly and immediately saw these brown and black clouds. I snuggled lower down into my bed. 'Go to sleep,' I ordered myself. But the clouds under my eyes were forming into a face. A face covered in darkness except for the eyes. Terrible purple eyes which bored into you. I shook my head. But the face just went on forming.

Finally I shot out of bed. What was I conjuring up now? I flung off my bedclothes. I was sweating like crazy. Then I stretched across for my hi-fi. Of course it wasn't there. I tried again. Still no sign of it. But even in this alien recreation of my room, it must be here somewhere.

Then suddenly I touched it, miles from where it usually was. I seized hold of it, then I put my headphones firmly over my ears. Some DJ was talking the usual rubbish. But while he was gabbing on, I felt safe. Nothing could happen to me now.

I fell asleep with my headphones on. When I woke up my alarm was ringing and my bedroom belonged to me again. Downstairs I could hear Mum filling the kettle. It was Saturday morning. Normally I'd be shooting off to work at Waitrose. But they 'had regretfully let me go' as they put it. With luck, I'd be taken on again for Christmas.

I needed the money. Running a car wasn't cheap. Still, this morning I could lie here and relax. Everything was safe, normal and dull. I smiled at the way I wound myself up last night. Then I felt ashamed, deeply ashamed. But that was the last time I would let it happen. I will never be afraid again.

CHAPTER 3

'I WAS TRAPPED'

I didn't think about the dark spirit all day. But as soon as I turned my light off that's all I could think about. Had I really seen it in that church? By day the idea seemed immature waffle. At night though, the idea took hold again. But this was so pathetic. I stared into the darkness, desperately trying to think about something else. But once you try and hide a thought it just finds another door to walk through. And another . . .

I groped my way out of bed and towards my bedside light. I switched the light on again and peered around the bedroom focusing on the little basic things like my socks and Batman boxer shorts on the floor. They were what was real. Nothing else.

I kept staring at them – and I left the light on. It seemed so puerile to still need to have a light on at seventeen. Besides I find it hard to sleep with artificial lights on. If only we didn't have to sleep. It's just a waste of time anyway. Someone should invent a drug that meant we didn't have to go to sleep. Then I could stay up all night, with lights on in every room and music blaring: that would be two fingers up at the darkness, wouldn't it?

I lay thinking about this for a while: me never sleeping – what a brilliant idea. Then somehow my thoughts switched to Louise. She kept popping up in my head, actually. But now I had a special reason for thinking about her as tomorrow night Angie has arranged for the four of us to got out for a drink. Normally I hate 'set-ups' like that. But this time I was prepared to go through with it. I was pretty amazed at myself. Not that I want to go out with Louise or anything. I'm just intrigued by her personality.

The next night we all met in the Yorkshire Grey, although Yorkshire Youth Club would be a more accurate name. It was crammed with people and took about three hours to get to the bar.

I felt quite awkward, though. It was as if Louise and I were on stage under all these glaring spotlights. It didn't seem natural.

And I felt as if I were giving a performance, trying to be funny and all that. I really wished I hadn't gone out with Louise like this; somehow it took all the subtlety away. I didn't even know what kind of impression I was making. Louise was quite jolly and friendly but I hadn't a clue what she thought of me. Somehow that little chat we'd had before – the one where she said I'd reminded her of Clint Eastwood – was more intimate than the whole of that evening.

Still, I suppose you have to go through these rituals and it did give me the courage to ring her up the next day and ask if she wanted to come out for a meal, 'as it was half-term'. What half-term had to do with it I don't know. But anyway Louise said she'd 'love to' – mad girl – and I picked up her at half past seven.

This time she was quite dressed up in dark trousers, a white blouse and a rich wine-coloured waistcoat. Seeing her like that gave me a real sense of pride. She'd dressed up for me. ME! I was glad I'd worn my only smart jacket.

In the restaurant my stomach, for some obscure reason, started making strange noises.

'I'm sorry for sounding like I swallowed a trombone player,' I said. She found that quite funny. Actually I made her laugh several times. And all through the meal I kept glancing over at her. I couldn't quite believe she was here with me. She was very charming but not in an artificial way. In fact she seemed as if she was in a kind of a dream, far away sometimes, but never distant. She was quite frank – she told me for instance that her dad had left home years ago and she only hears from him on her birthday and at Christmas now. Yet she was mysterious too. I liked that; I mean, nothing's more boring than a girl who tells you her life story in four seconds.

'Doing anything special tomorrow night?' I asked.

'I've got a rehearsal.'

'Rehearsal?'

'Yeah, I've just joined the Shaw players.'

If there was one thing I hated it was amateur dramatics. From my experience they were peopled by pretentious snobs.

'So are you into acting and all that stuff?'

She smiled. 'When I was younger all I wanted was to be an actress. I did some acting for a while. But I really wasn't very good.'

'Miss Modesty.'

'No. I mean, I wasn't terrible. But I never . . . I'd see some girls and they'd just light up the stage. And afterwards they'd be so high. I remember this girl telling me that out on the stage she could get rid of everything that was bothering her. I could never do that.' She looked away. 'Still, I thought I'd give it another go, now I'm older. We'll see. But I'll be finished by nine, or just after. So we could go for a drink, if you like.'

'I'd like,' I said.

The next night I sat on the steps by the double-doors, watching the drama group stream out. They were all together in one big gaggle. All the girls, apart from Louise, were wearing floral skirts and those furry little boots that Oliver Twist used to wear. The guys were in denim and either had really long hair or skinhead haircuts. Louise saw me and waved. She was about to come over when this guy in a big woolly jumper said, 'Don't be ashamed of what happened tonight, will you?'

Louise shook her head, sadly. 'I messed up, I'm sorry I did.' Then she ran over to me.

As soon as we were out of earshot I asked, 'What was woolly jumper waffling on about?'

'Rich, I should never have gone there,' she began.

'I think you need a drink,' I said.

27

Tonight, The Yorkshire Grey was pretty empty. We got a table in the corner right away. I asked, 'Come on then, what terrible deed have you done?'

She stared down at her drink. 'You'll think I'm mad.'

'No I won't, tell me.'

She gave me one of her smiles. 'We started tonight by doing this exercise where you had to empty your mind – that didn't take me long! Then Simon said, "I want you to keep your eyes closed but imagine you are in this room which is covered in darkness. Now slowly feel your way around the room." So I did that all right.' She shook her head. 'I still can't believe I did this. Anyway, Simon said, "There is a door. I want you to find this door and then open your eyes. But only open your eyes when you've seen the door." Well, that was my problem. I couldn't find the door anywhere. And in the end I called out, "I can't find the door" and he was saying, "Yes you can. There is a door, a big wide door."

'I know it sounds stupid but I was going crazy now. For I was running around and around that room, telling myself I'd got to find the door. And I wanted to see it so badly. But it was no good.' She looked up at me, her eyes suddenly wide with fear. 'There was no door there, Rich. I swear there wasn't. So there was no way I could get out of that room. I was trapped.' She paused. 'So in the end I screamed because I – I don't know why.' She gave a kind of half-laugh. 'It was a loud scream too. That has to be the most embarrassing moment in my life. Why couldn't I find that door?' Suddenly, she was staring directly at me.

'Maybe you were looking for it too hard.'

'You reckon?'

'I know, when I'm feeling pressurised, I can't do anything.'

'Yes, that's true.' She seemed unexpectedly relieved. 'You're right.'

'I usually am,' I said. 'Just call me the oracle. So anyway, what was the point of that exercise?'

'It was a warm-up for our next production.'

'Which is?'

'*Dick Whittington*.'

I stared at her disbelievingly, then sniggered. '*Dick Whittington*? All that hassle just to say, "Behind you" and "Oh no he's not"? The way they were going on, I thought you were doing *Hamlet* at least.'

She laughed. 'I'm glad I told you. I don't think I'll go back though. Drama brings too much out.' She seemed suddenly afraid. Then it was as if she saw me again and she gave me this really warm look, just as if she liked me a lot. I tell you, that look killed me. And driving home afterwards it just kept flashing through my head. Somehow, I didn't want to let it go.

I must have been raving on about Louise to my mum because she invited her round for tea the next day. My dad was in one of his silly moods and actually raced me to the door when Louise rang.

To my horror he won too. Louise gazed at this panting man; bald on the top of his head with grey around the sides, round face, large glasses.

29

'Oh, hi,' she began.

'Oh, low,' he replied. To my dad that was humour.

I rescued Louise and formally introduced them. Then my mum ran past. My mum was one of those people who always seemed to be busy. My dad just flopped about the house but my mum was always taking someone to the hospital or raising money for some cause or doing something in the garden. She paused long enough to have a little chat with Louise and I could tell my mum liked her. I was pleased about that, even though I don't really care what my parents think about my friends.

Then, after tea we were sitting in the lounge, and my dad was being jolly – sometimes I think he'd have made a great Father Christmas – when I went out to the kitchen to make some more coffee (I'm so domesticated) and my mum followed me.

'You've got yourself a nice girlfriend there.'

'She's not my girlfriend,' I said at once. At the moment she was just a girl I liked who intrigued me. I didn't know if I wanted to get involved: well part of me did, very much. After all, look what happened last time. I got sucked in by it all. I really believed I'd found a girl for life. I trusted her totally.

But Louise was different. Or was she? I liked her a lot but did I really know her? Best not to get too involved. I must keep something of myself back this time. I thought again of my last girlfriend and the night I saw her down the pub with that fish. I just stood there, watching them blow my insides away. I never want to go through that again.

I never will.

Still, the next night I did go round to Louise's house for a meal. It was a horrible evening with dirty, grey fog swirling all around me. Everything seemed blurred, disguised, confused. No wonder the guy on the radio was advising everyone to stay at home. But I couldn't go back now. I drove blindly on. Everything familiar was vanishing before my eyes. Now, nothing was real except the fog blowing furiously against my window.

By the time I'd found Louise's house I was nearly an hour late. As soon as I got out of the car I shuddered, without knowing why. I decided it was the fog. I hated the way it clung on to you, smothering your face with its stale smell. It reminded me of the darkness in my bedroom. The darkness that somehow I'd overpowered last night. Well, I hadn't woken up anyway. Any dark spirits that were lurking last night would have been playing to an empty house. I wasn't giving my monster a chance to show itself. That's what I called the dark spirit now; my monster. Somehow that helped distance it, lessen its power. I could almost laugh at it when I called it 'my monster'. Almost. Then I heard my name being called and there was Louise running towards me.

'Oh look, it's Mr Intrepid,' she said, grinning. Then she gave me this big hug and said, 'We never thought you'd get through – you're a bit of a hero.'

'That's true . . . So how are you?'

'All right, except for the fact my mum managed to turn my red shirt pink by putting it in the wash with loads of white stuff. We've had a bit of a heated discussion about that.'

'I don't know, you'll probably look quite nice in pink.'

'Thank you.' Then she asked mock-indignantly, 'And why are you sticking up for my mum?'

'I don't know. I like people's mums and their grandparents. I often play poker with Danny's grandad. I'm going to see my Nan tomorrow. It's her birthday. She's about a thousand.'

'I'd like to meet her.'

'Would you really?' She nodded. 'Come along tomorrow then, great.'

'Anyway, my mum is dying to meet you.'

Louise opened the lounge door and said 'Mum, meet Rich.'

The first shock was that her mum was blonde. I hadn't been expecting that. She also had blue eyes, not green, like Louise's.

'Richard, you must have had a terrible journey.'

'Not too bad . . . Sorry I'm late.'

'Oh, don't worry about that.' She gazed around her. She looked slightly distracted. 'Sit down, make yourself at home. You must be hungry. It's all ready, isn't it?' She turned to Louise.

'Practically,' said Louise. 'I'll just go and see.'

Her mum sat down. 'You don't smoke, do you?'

'No, gave up a year ago now.'

'I wish I could. But I seem to need the evil weed. Louise is always going on at me. She even makes me put on this wretched air filter every time I light up.' She looked around. 'Where is it? I swear it moves.' She went over, switched on the air-filter and sat down again.

'Louise was telling me you're the deputy head at Wycliffe Primary,' I said.

'That's right.' She leant back. 'Every summer I say, that's it, I'm going to do something else. It's the pupils that keep me there. I love their imaginations, like today . . .' Then she rattled on about this essay an eight-year-old had written about the countryside, while I tried to figure out what was missing in this room. There was something. At last I decided what it was: photographs.

Most people have a few family snaps in their lounge, don't they. There were no photographs at all, but shelves and shelves of books.

Louise put her head round the door. 'Come and get it . . . and no smoking at the dinner table.'

'What would you do with such a bossy daughter?'

Louise's mum stared around for an ashtray, as if she'd never been in this room before.

Over the meal, too, her mum seemed permanently distracted, but in an appealing way. There was a sense of fun about her face. And when you spoke about something, she was interested, her face lit up, just like Louise's. There was something warm and very approachable about her. Yet, when she wasn't smiling, there was pain in her eyes, too.

After offering to help with the washing up (I know how to get mums to like me) I returned to the lounge with Louise.

'Your mum's great,' I said.

'Did she tell you about her school?'

'Oh, yes.'

'My mum's so dedicated, very, very dedicated.' Louise said this almost sadly. Then, for a moment the conversation went dead. I felt Louise was saying something else, but I wasn't sure. So instead, I got up and pretended to be studying the books.

'You've got a lot of books here, but have you got my favourite?'

She stood up. 'What's that?'

'It's a totally wild book called, *The History of English Plant Pots*. You must have read it.'

'I've got it upstairs, actually.'

'Fascinating, isn't it?'

'Yes, it is, but not quite as fascinating as my favourite, *Nodding Dogs Through the Ages*.'

'I'd kill for a copy of that.'

She gave a soft laugh, then said, 'Shall I put some music on?'

'Definitely.'

'How about Suzanne Vega?'

'Mmm.'

'You don't like her?'

'Oh yeah, I really love people who wallow in their sorrows and write deep and meaningful songs about people standing outside cafés – great.' I smiled. 'I'm afraid I'm really opinionated about music.'

'Do you play?'

'The guitar. How original, you say.'

'Would you like to play professionally?'

'That's my dream – or one of them. I want a three-piece band. Something that's really tight.

I don't like those bands where everyone tries to hog the limelight. I think you should just be enjoying the music. And three-pieces are always good: Cream, Jimi Hendrix Experience, The Jam, even The Cure started out as a three-piece . . .' I stopped. 'Normally, when I start talking about music people run away.'

'But why, I think it's interesting.'

'You're the only one who does,' I began, and she was staring at me very intently now. Maybe she did like me. But I found that difficult to believe. She was beautiful. She could be spending time with real hunks: not me, a music obsessed dreamer who's still scared of the dark.

'So, how about you?' I asked. 'What are your deep, dark ambitions?'

'I haven't got any, really.'

'That surprises me.'

'No, my motto is, "expect nothing". So I expect nothing,' she smiled, 'but secretly I hope for a lot.'

'We all do really,' I said. 'No one wants to have a pointless life.'

'Sometimes I think I'm going to have an amazing life. I feel it's all ahead of me, just waiting, you know.' I nodded. 'Other times I'm not so sure.'

'How do you mean?'

Her voice sank. 'I'm not so sure I'll even be around.'

'You'd better be. I want someone to come and see my band.'

'Okay. I'll stay around for that.'

But I noticed she was shivering. 'What are you going on about anyway – will you be around?'

'It's just sometimes . . .' She looked away, then said, 'But I'm definitely coming to see your band. I'll be in the front row, okay?' She touched my face. Then my arms slid around her neck as we kissed, one of those kisses that stretch into infinity.

Later, Louise's mum returned to watch the news, the first half of which was taken up with all the accidents that had occurred in the fog. A seriously bearded guy then intoned, 'The AA advise all motorists to stay off the roads tonight.' He rambled on while I wondered how I was going to get back.

'We can't let Rich go back in this, can we, Mum?' said Louise.

'No, of course not,' said her mum.

'Honestly, it doesn't matter. I haven't got that far to go.'

For a long second there was silence, as Louise and her mum looked at each other, then her mum said, firmly, 'No, Richard, we've got a spare room – and you must use it.' Then she looked across again at Louise, as if needing reassurance before going on, 'I'll just go and tidy the room up for you, it hasn't been used for a while.'

'Do you want a hand?' asked Louise.

'Won't take a minute,' said her mum, briskly. 'Don't forget to ring your family, will you, Richard?'

After she'd left, I said, 'This is a real nuisance, isn't it?'

'Of course not.' But Louise seemed apprehensive, uncertain. And I felt excluded, somehow.

Her mum came down again. She rubbed her hands together, smiling nervously. 'I think the room is fit for habitation now. I've slipped a hot water bottle into the bed. But you must let me know if you need anything.'

'Thanks very much,' I said.

'You're welcome,' replied her mum. 'Actually, it will be good to have the room used again.'

Louise took me upstairs. I was expecting something small and anonymous, like an hotel room. But this room belonged to someone. It was a boy's room. A boy of about six or seven, I'd say, from the photographs of him grinning in his baseball cap. And there was his desk, with a mug full of crayons and fat marker pens. On the window-ledge were rows of dinosaurs, a policeman's helmet and that baseball cap, while his bed had covers with turtles on. It was quite a high bed, like a bunk bed, and had a little ladder beside it.

This room told me so much about him. But where was he? And why hadn't Louise ever mentioned him? I looked across at Louise's face – and then I knew why.

CHAPTER 4

THE NIGHT FOR BAD DREAMS

'Is he?' I couldn't say the word.

'It was flu, that's all it was,' said Louise, 'only he couldn't shake it off, just got worse and worse. Then the doctor said his heart was involved, said he had a heart condition.' Her voice sank. Suddenly, she sounded weary. 'But that was rubbish, because Ben was so active, always bouncing his ball around you or asking you to take him down the park. And even when he was in hospital, he asked for a drawing pad.' She picked up the pad on the little table by his bed. 'Even then, he was sitting up in bed, drawing these pictures . . . he was always on the go, never ill.'

She put the pad carefully back on the table. Behind us, the fog was pressing against the window. It was like a great tide rolling in, taking away everything we knew with it. Suddenly, I hated that fog. Why couldn't we stop it, make it disappear. I didn't want to see it pushing against the window, searching for a way into this room. As if she could read my thoughts, Louise went over and drew down the dark brown blind. Then she looked up at me, shivering slightly.

I asked, 'How long ago did Ben . . .?'

'We lost Ben a long time ago . . . over a year now.'

That really shocked me. This room felt as if Ben had only left it a few weeks before. It still seemed to be waiting for him.

'Somehow, we've never got around to throwing any of his things out. Mum and I have tried a few times, but it didn't seem right, somehow. So it's all here, just as it was. We hardly ever use this room now. Mum cleans it, of course, but otherwise . . . you don't mind sleeping here, do you, Rich?'

'No, I like this room,' I said firmly. And I did. I also felt this great rush of feeling for Louise – and her mum. What a terrible, wasteful, nasty thing to lose a brother so young. It must have been so horrible for her – and her parents. Yet there was also this shrill, indignant voice in my head, which kept asking, 'So why didn't she tell me she had a brother? How could she not tell me something as important as that?' I brushed away that indignant voice and said, 'I wish I'd met Ben.'

'He drove you mad sometimes,' said Louise, 'but everyone liked him. It was hard not to like him. That's why it doesn't make any sense, does it?'

'No, it doesn't,' I said, quietly. Then I took her in my arms and we held each other so tightly I could feel her heart pounding against my chest. We held on to each other until her mum called her.

Louise said, 'I'm glad you're here. I know Ben would have liked you, too.'

Then I was alone. Yet I felt like a trespasser, because Ben was in every corner of this room. There, in the chest of drawers by the door, were all his clothes, with his pyjamas neatly folded on top. Another cupboard had all his toys in it, while every wall was crammed with his posters of Spurs players and his drawings (they were a bit like the ones I used to draw, full of stick-people with massive heads).

I gazed at his photograph, dark blue eyes, snub nose, sticky-out ears, very short hair and a really mischievous grin. I could see why everyone liked him. Then I spotted a letter from Louise to him, stuck on to his mirror. It said: *Dear Ben, I am writing to you because you say you never get any letters. I think you are a great boy and maybe I will take you swimming today. And tonight I will read you another story. Lots of love. Louise XXXX*

It was all here: everything of Ben's, except Ben himself.

I sat down on the bed. There was a gap between the bed and the table beside it: it was too small for an adult to go through but a child could squeeze in there and hide away from everyone.

When I was younger I'd have hidden in there. And suddenly I knew Ben had hidden in that gap too. I could see him curled up in there, laughing softly, as everyone searched madly for him.

And even as I switched off the light I lay thinking about Ben, feeling a real sense of loss that I'd never meet him. He'd have been a great younger brother. I sometimes imagined I had a younger brother and was taking him to see Spurs and telling him about music (good music). And Ben seemed so close to me, so real, it was hard to believe he'd vanished from this earth, forever.

But – and this is really important – I didn't find his room eerie at all. Instead, I felt just as if I'd stepped back ten years and discovered someone whom I knew would have been a good mate. I didn't feel like an imposter any more. I belonged in this room or rather my younger self did. So when I went to sleep I wasn't scared at all. That makes what happened later all the more strange.

I drifted off to sleep easily. I may have woken up once. I'm not sure. What I do remember is waking up much later that night because I was freezing cold. This was odd because earlier, if anything, I'd been a bit too hot. I opened my eyes and saw a dark shape by the door. But I didn't panic. How often had I woken up in my own bedroom and seen a sinister shape, which turned out to be a coat hanging on the door, or clothes flung over a chair.

So then I closed my eyes again. You're in a strange room I told myself. There will be a rational explanation for this. Then I thought of one: Ben had a basketball net on the back of his door. That was what I'd seen.

Reassured, I opened my eyes again and saw something move. It shot right across the room. I was terrified. What was in here? I didn't know. I just had to get out. I HAD TO GET OUT.

I jumped out of bed, quite forgetting how high up I was, and fell on to the floor. I scrambled to my feet, running towards what I thought was the door. Instead, I crashed against the chest of drawers, sending a clock and some toys flying. I ran around the room, madly. Where was the door? I couldn't find the door. There was no way out of here. I was trapped. Someone get me out of here, please. I groped my way forward then froze. What was that? There it was again, a sharp knocking sound. Then there was a tiny click as the door slowly opened. Seconds ago, that door wasn't there. I swear it wasn't.

'Richard, are you all right?' Louise's mum was standing there.

I cowered in front of her, in just my boxer shorts. 'There was something in here, I saw it move,' I cried.

Louise's mum just stared at me. 'I think maybe you had a nightmare,' she said, gently. I knew it wasn't a nightmare. But I didn't argue. Suddenly, I felt foolish.

Louise's mum switched on the light. At once, Ben took over: the room was full of him again. Then she said kindly, 'I know about nightmares, they can be very real, can't they?' She bent down and picked up the clock.

'Sorry about that,' I said.

She just smiled faintly, then she started picking up Ben's toys, which had fallen too.

I slunk back towards the bed. 'What a mess,' I said, with an embarrassed laugh.

'That's all right,' she replied, but I noticed how carefully she put each toy back. 'Now, can I get you a drink or anything?' she asked.

'No, honestly, I'm just sorry I woke you up.' It was then I heard footsteps. Someone was walking very slowly up the stairs. Then I saw Louise walk past my room. The door was wide open and she must have noticed the lights but she didn't look in, didn't appear to even see me.

'Is that Louise?'

'Yes,' her mother gave a rather uncertain laugh. 'It must be the night for bad dreams. I took her downstairs, gave her some hot milk. Then I heard you and . . . the nightmare must have jumped out of her head and into yours. I hope it's not my turn now.' She gave another uncertain smile. 'Are you sure I can't get you a hot drink?'

'No, thanks . . . Louise. She is all right?'

'Oh yes, it's just nightmares cast such a shadow, don't they? It takes a while to lose them. Anyway, I really do wish you pleasant dreams. Shall I leave the light on?'

I hesitated. It sounded so wimpish to say, 'Yes,' but as if understanding this, Louise's mum said, 'I'll leave it on for now, then. Goodnight, Richard.'

'Goodnight,' I said.

The door clicked behind her. Then I looked up at the light. The shade had turtles all over it. It seemed so innocent, so silly. Yet, tonight, in this house . . . It must be the night for bad dreams: that's what Louise's mum said. I thought of Louise and her nightmare. I wonder what she'd dreamt about. And how strange she hadn't seen me.

But what I'd seen in this room; no, that wasn't any kind of dream, was it? I'd definitely seen something move. A dark shape. The spirit I'd brought back from Abbotts Hill. The Spirit of Death.

It's funny, these last nights I thought I'd lost him. But all the time the spirit had been hiding, waiting for the right moment to show itself. Where was it now? Had it dissolved into the darkness again?

Now I was being silly, irrational. But all the same . . . I looked across at Ben, still grinning away in his baseball cap. Ben, I brought something into your room tonight – and I don't know what it is.

CHAPTER 5

'IT HAS WON'

'So in the morning, you didn't see Louise at all?'
Angie sounded amazed.

'No,' I replied. 'I hung about as long as I could
after breakfast and there still wasn't any sign of her.
Louise's mum did offer to wake her. But I said,
just ask her to ring me later. We're supposed to be
going to my nan's birthday rave-up tonight.'

'And she didn't ring?' asked Angie.

'I hung around all day as well. I mean, I can
understand her not wanting to go round my nan's.
But it was she who offered to go.'

'So why can't you ring her?' asked Angie.

'I don't want to look as if I'm pushing it,' I said.

'Aaah, poor Richard,' said Angie, mock-sym-
pathetically. Angie was always trying to get me
to confide in her. She'd say, in her best sisterly
manner, 'So Rich, is there a woman in your life?'
Normally I don't indulge her. But tonight I was so
confused, I thought a girl's perspective might be
useful, especially as Angie and Louise were friends.

We were round at Angie's house, actually. Her
parents were away – they often went away – and

45

when they did, Danny just moved in. I knew I'd never see him on those days. In just a few months, he and Angie had turned into an old married couple. He was upstairs in Angie's room now, getting ready. Except, it was their room now. They were so intimate, while I . . . I could never imagine getting that close to a girl.

'Something else happened last night, didn't it?' said Angie. I looked up at her in some amazement. I hadn't told Angie anything about last night's 'nightmares'.

'Well . . .' I hesitated.

She pounced. 'Come on, it did. You must tell me everything.' She was sprawled out on the sofa, while I was picking at the rug by the fire.

'All right, Auntie Angie.' She laughed. She loved that. 'But this is going to sound mighty weird.'

'Even better.'

'You know I told you I slept in Ben's room.'

'Louise's dead brother's room,' said Angie.

'Yeah, that's right. Anyway, in the night I woke up – and I was definitely awake – and I saw a dark shape by the door.'

'Probably just a coat,' interrupted Angie.

'Don't cut me off in my prime,' I said.

'Sorry,' she replied. 'Go on.'

'I was about to say, I wasn't too perturbed. Like you, I thought there's bound to be a rational explanation, but then suddenly, the shape moved. In fact, it ran right across the room.' My voice rose, 'I saw it move, just as clearly as I'm seeing you.'

'Wind–up,' called Danny from upstairs.

But Angie just stared at me incredulously, then asked slowly, 'So what was it?'

'I don't know. It was just a dark shape, like a silhouette, it happened so fast.'

Angie sat up, hunching her shoulders together. 'Rich, is this true?'

Danny called down again, 'It's a wind-up.'

I said, 'It is true, Angie. I swear.'

'I don't like the sound of this,' she said. 'I wish you hadn't told me now.'

'You asked me,' I cried.

'I know. Did you tell Louise?'

'Well, that's the other strange thing. Now, do you want to hear this?'

'I'm not sure,' said Angie. 'No, go on. Of course I do.'

'When I saw the thing move I was ready to run for my life. Instead, I went crashing into this cupboard, sent one of the clocks flying and Louise's mum came in.'

'Just a bit embarrassing.'

I nodded. 'She thought I was having a nightmare. Anyway, she was leaving, when I saw Louise coming up the stairs and Louise saw me but didn't react at all. It was like she was in some kind of trance.'

'You are making this up,' cried Angie.

'I swear I'm not.'

'But that's why she hasn't rung you, then. She's too embarrassed.'

'You reckon?'

'Yes. I mean, if a new boyfriend saw me walking up the stairs in the middle of the night in a trance,

47

I'd be . . . She must have been sleep-walking. Wouldn't it have been funny if she'd slept-walked her way into your room.' She gave a wicked laugh. 'And now you say it, I do remember hearing about her brother. Miss Minkin, our form-teacher, told us. But when Louise came back she never spoke about it and I guess we just forgot. Isn't that awful? She was going out with Scott Flynn then. He used to write her all these soppy love poems. Do you know him?'

'I know him,' I said grimly. 'He's a very obvious kind of person and just about the biggest fashion victim to walk this earth. How long did she go out with him?'

'Oh, not long,' said Angie. 'And actually, he finished it. He said – that's right – he said Louise played her cards too close to her chest.'

'That's rubbish. She's one of the most warm, open people . . .' I stopped.

Angie was laughing at me. 'I knew it wouldn't last between Louise and Scott. Louise was only filling in time with him. He was just a stand-in. But when I saw you two, I knew you'd be brilliant together.'

'How?'

'Oh, just by looking at your eyes and your hand movements and the way you kept touching her shoulder and being protective of her when we were at Abbotts Hill. And by the way Louise kept smiling at you . . . I'm never wrong about these things, you know.'

I couldn't help flushing with pleasure after hearing this. But then I demanded, 'So why hasn't she rung me, then? She doesn't want to see me tonight, that's why.'

Angie gave me a coy smile. 'Girls can't appear too eager, that's all. So ring her.' I hesitated. 'Go on, ring her.' She got up and brought the phone over to me. 'You know you want to, really.'

I grabbed the receiver and started dialling Louise's number. If she blew me out, she blew me out, I said to myself. Louise answered. 'Hello.' Her voice sounded blurred, sleepy.

'Hi, it's Rich.'

'Oh, hi Rich.' Life seemed to flow back into her voice.

'How are you?'

She went on, 'Not bad. I was wondering when you were going to ring me about tonight. I thought you might be catching up on some sleep. I'm sorry Ben's room gave you nightmares.'

'No, it wasn't Ben's room,' and, I wanted to add, 'it wasn't any nightmare either.' Instead, I said, 'You had a bit of a nightmare too.'

There was a sharp intake of breath before she said softly, 'It wasn't exactly a nightmare. It was nothing at all really, just me being silly. So anyway, are we still on for tonight, then?'

'Yeah, sure. I mean, we needn't stay at my nan's too long. I'm dropping Angie and Danny off at a concert at Bowes House and we can always join them there, later.'

'Yeah, whatever. I'm easy.' She gave her familiar laugh and for the first time I felt us both relaxing a bit.

'See you in about an hour, then,' I said.

49

'Bye, Rich. Take care,' she said. I put the phone down.

'You didn't blow her a kiss,' said Danny, smirking in the doorway.

I went over and started ruffling his hair. 'It doesn't look any different to when you went up,' I said.

Danny pushed my hand away. 'Yes, it does. There are no pieces flapping about now, or at least there weren't. Are we ready to rave, then?'

'I've just got to go to the little girls' room,' said Angie.

'Well, hurry up,' said Danny. 'We don't want to miss the start.'

'We've been ready for ages,' said Angie, speeding past him.

'Seeing Louise again tonight? Getting serious, is it?' Danny gave me his familiar, teasing smile.

'No, not at all,' I said.

He sat down on the sofa. 'So you saw a dark shape running past you, doing the marathon, was it? Did it have jogging shorts on?'

'All right. All right.'

He looked at me curiously. 'You were spinning Angie your yarn again. Weren't you?'

'Actually, I wasn't. No.'

Danny looked at me. 'I never believe anything you say.' Then he added, 'But I knew we shouldn't have gone to Abbotts Hill. Harry said if we weren't careful . . .'

'Don't bring your medium into this,' I interrupted.

'All right, but we were messing in things we

50

'shouldn't,' began Danny. Then Angie came back downstairs and we changed the subject.

I dropped Danny and Angie off at Bowes House and said I might see them later. Then I picked Louise up.

On the way to my nan's I only mentioned the previous night once. Louise immediately froze up, so I let it drop. We ended up talking quite a lot about my nan. I wanted to prepare Louise.

'My nan used to be so active,' I said. 'She walked everywhere, carried everything herself. For instance, once this guy came to her door, wanting to buy antiques. She said she had nothing to sell but he wouldn't budge. So in the end she chased him right down the road. The neighbours still talk about that. She was about eighty then. But last year she fell on to her hip and went into hospital, had this big operation, still got the scars on her face. She's not been well at all lately. We needn't stay long,' I added.

'How old is she today?' asked Louise.

'Eighty-seven,' I said. 'I haven't seen her for a while. Well, the last time I saw her she had put all these tins in the cupboard, "in case we have another war". And half the tins were out of date anyway. Seeing her do that depressed the hell out of me. She didn't seem like herself any more.' I gave a kind of half-laugh, then said, 'We'll only stay for five minutes.'

My nan lived in a bungalow right on the edge of town. For as long as I'd known her, she'd lived there. My Uncle David opened the door. He shook hands with me, exchanged nervous smiles with Louise and explained that Aunt Marion had stayed at home because she was still getting over flu and my two cousins were hoping to pop in later this week. Then Mum and Dad appeared from the kitchen. They looked so pleased to see me I felt a stab of guilt; had they really thought I wouldn't turn up?

'She's so looking forward to seeing you,' said Mum. 'Been talking about nothing else.'

I hesitated. When I was younger, I'd just run into the lounge where Nan would be sitting in her rocking chair. I'd rush into her arms, then after the hugs I'd get down to the main business of the day: eating. There was always so much food at Nan's house and proper food too: cakes, sweets, biscuits. Her kitchen always smelt so exciting. No wonder I loved Nan so much.

Nan, who was always on my side and would say, 'You come and sit by me,' whenever I was upset. Nan, who would always listen to my troubles. Nan, whom I haven't seen since Christmas Day.

I opened the lounge door. There was the same sweet, musty smell. But this room was different now. In the past it had been a bright, friendly room, with its flowery wallpaper, busy carpet, enjoyably naffo clock with loads of sea-shells on it and a large television babbling away in the corner. Now, even the light from the television hurt Nan's eyes and the dim darkness of the room somehow magnified the heavy furniture. Nothing stirred except for the imposter in the rocking chair; a skinny, shrunken figure in a red dressing gown. That wasn't my nan. My nan was a large woman who always liked

52

to dress up; she'd spend hours going through the catalogues with Mum.

The imposter raised up two tiny little claws to me. The skin on her hands was all loose and sagging and shook until I took hold of them. Then, a tiny slither of light came into those misty blue-grey eyes. 'You're a good boy,' she chanted. She leant over and took a deep sniff of the chrysanthemums beside her. The ones I'd sent her this morning. 'He never forgets how much I like flowers.' She was addressing Louise, smiling vaguely.

'Nan, this is Louise.'

'Oh, yes,' said Nan, as if she'd been expecting her. 'Bit cold tonight, isn't it, Louise? I've got some chocolate pudding in the kitchen. Would you like some, dear?'

'Oh, yes I would,' said Louise.

Nan's face lit up. 'You look like you need feeding up. You both do.' She made as if to push herself up.

'I'll get it, Nan,' I said, hastily.

In the kitchen, Mum and Dad had just finished washing up. Uncle David was talking to the nurse who came in to 'look after' Nan. It seemed very crowded with the five of us. In the old days, Nan would never have let us all hang around her kitchen like this. I was only allowed in to raid the pantry, which was crammed with cakes, pies and biscuits and a bottle of diarrhoea tablets on the top shelf.

Then the kitchen had been like a little kingdom. Tonight, it just seemed cramped and ordinary and only smelt of soap and washing-up liquid. I took two slices of the chocolate cake – which no one else had touched – and went back into the lounge. Louise was sprawled at Nan's feet, while Nan was staying, 'Yes, my hair was nearly as thick as yours, my dear. But I had to cut if off.'

'But why?' asked Louise.

'Because we didn't have any wood for the fire, so we burnt it.' She gave a surprisingly strong laugh. 'I was so upset, seeing my lovely hair on the fire.' She patted her wispy, white hair, then reached out and touched Louise's hair. 'My hair was just like yours,' she said.

I knelt down beside Louise as Nan told her all the old family stories. I'd heard them many times before, but not for a while. Every so often she'd stop and smile, as if she were warming herself on a particular memory. And occasionally, she'd look at us eating her chocolate cake and nod approvingly. 'My recipe,' she'd murmur. And then she started telling stories about me, when I was little. 'He'd get on this rocking chair and rock so fast, well I was frightened he was going to go through my glass door.'

I had a sudden flash of memory as I saw myself rocking furiously and Nan rushing in . . . And now that little incident is part of Nan's memories too, a vast tapestry, stretching back over eighty years. I looked around at all the old photographs: Mum and Dad on their wedding day; Nan with her parents; Nan, my mum and dad and me on holiday in Brighton. Nan was the one constant figure, binding the generations together. Nan had always seemed old to me. But then she looked comfortable, solid. Now, suddenly, Time was rushing at her, tugging furiously at her face, her arms, her legs. Until, well, look at her – withering away like an apple that's been left in the bowl too long.

She closed her eyes and Mum said from the doorway, 'I expect Nan would like to rest now.' To my surprise, Nan heard this. She half-opened her eyes and gazed around her, looking suddenly dazed, as if she wasn't quite sure who we were.

'We'll let you have a rest now, Nan,' I said.

'Yes, I'm so tired. I've worked hard all my life, you see. I'm eighty-seven, you know.' She was talking to us as if we were strangers. But then a glimmer of recognition came back into her face. 'He doesn't eat enough,' she said to Louise.

Louise smiled, and said, gently, 'It's been lovely meeting you and hearing all your stories.'

'And so lovely meeting you.' A pause. An agonising pause. Nan looked up into the air, as if Louise's name was floating there, just out of reach.

'Louise,' she whispered.

But Nan didn't seem to hear, instead she said, 'My head . . . my head is full of holes.' She closed her eyes. 'My poor head,' she murmured.

Ruthlessly, mercilessly, Time was unravelling everything that made Nan, Nan. And there was nothing we could do. Soon she would be all unstitched. I felt a wave of such anger and pain, it struck my head like a blow. I got up, whispered, 'Goodbye Nan,' but I don't think she heard me. So I just kissed her gently. Behind me I heard Louise saying her goodbyes. I turned to her, 'Can we go for a quick walk? My head's buzzing.'

Louise nodded. Then she slipped her hand in mine. We walked for ages, crunching our way through all the dead leaves, while Louise let me ramble on about Nan.

Then, finally, we went back to the car and I drove Louise to my house.

'This has been a rubbish evening for you, hasn't it?' I asked.

'No.' She sounded indignant. 'I really liked your nan and the way she spoke to me, as if she'd known me for years. She was so warm and friendly.'

'You're just saying that. You've had a really heavy evening, but now I'm going to make it up to you, you'll see.'

I steamed into my house, put some loud music tapes on and cracked open a bottle of wine. 'I can't drink much. But you can.' And I kept filling Louise's glass up.

'You don't want to see me when I'm drunk,' said Louise, 'because I get really embarrassing.'

'Excellent.'

'No, honestly, my voice gets very high and I go round telling everyone I love them.'

'Sounds all right to me,' I said.

She bent over to put her glass on the table and then froze. 'There's Ben's pad.'

For a second, I froze too. I began, 'That's right. Your mum . . .'

'I know,' she told me. 'It just gave me a bit of a shock suddenly seeing it here.' She picked it up. 'Mum must have really liked you to give you this.'

'I was amazed she did,' I said. 'Your mum brought me in a cup of tea this morning when

I was looking at Ben's pad. I just said how good the drawings were and she said, "please take it". I thought she was just being polite at first, but she kept on saying, "I know Ben would be so proud you liked his drawings." '

'It's good she spoke to you about Ben. She hardly ever does now,' said Louise. 'He loved this pad. Took it to hospital with him. I gave it to him.'

'He's drawn a picture of you, hasn't he?'

'That's right.' Louise smiled again at the picture. It was a drawing of a grinning Louise playing the guitar. Underneath he had printed, MY ROKEING SIS.

'I didn't know you played the guitar.'

'Very badly. I was really flattered by that picture. Ben used to tell all his friends he had a cool sister. I don't know why.' She turned over the pages. 'He was getting so good at drawing too. I mean, look at this one of a train he saw. He was even beginning to show perspective. He really had so much talent. That's why what happened wasn't natural. There's no meaning to it.' She snapped the pad shut and downed the rest of her glass of wine.

'More?'

'Yes. Yes,' she said. Soon she was getting pretty merry and we were both giggling away at these pathetic jokes I told, while the shadows inched around us.

Finally, she asked, 'What time is it, Rich?'

I squinted at my watch. 'Late.'

'I know that,' she giggled. 'How late?'

'Something to one.'

'My mum will be freaking out.'

'She'll probably be fast asleep.'

'No, she always waits up,' she said, simply. Then she got up.

'You could stay,' I said. I didn't quite know what I was suggesting.

'Yes, I could,' said Louise.

I gave a little shiver of excitement. 'I'd like you to stay,' I said.

A light came into her eyes. 'Would you?' she said.

Into my mind flashed this image, of me waking up, with my arms around Louise. We were wrapped together so closely, so securely. And I felt a wave of such aching, longing.

'Don't go,' I whispered. She stared at me. I felt as if I were casting a spell over her, over both of us. 'You can ring up your mum. She won't know . . .' I let the rest of that sentence hang in the air. Then I smiled at her. I'd never felt so stirred, so alive. Life was suddenly flooded with meaning. Boldly now, I went on, 'My parents probably won't be back for ages yet.'

'Your parents,' echoed Louise.

And then I knew I'd broken the spell. The truth was, my parents could burst in at any moment. I was amazed they weren't home by now, actually. But I didn't want to think about any of that. So I persisted. 'Don't go.'

She gave me a very sweet smile, got up in a kind of slow motion, and picked up her coat from over the chair.

I drove her home.

When I got back, I expected signs of my parents' return. Instead, the answer-phone was flashing dementedly. I knew it wasn't going to be good news. My mum's voice came through. 'Hello Richard. This is just to let you know that we're staying over at Nan's tonight. Nothing to worry about and we'll see you bright and early tomorrow. Bye.'

I stood thinking about the message. Mum's tone had been too reassuring. There was something to worry about. Nan. Poor Nan. What has happened now? I wished Mum had told me. Then I had another thought. Louise could have stayed over tonight after all, so I needn't have taken her home. If only Mum had rung earlier, then Louise would be here now.

I had a mad urge to ring Louise. I even picked up the receiver. I wanted Louise to be here with me, so much. I didn't want to be alone. Especially tonight. Those last two words just slipped out.

Especially tonight.

I put the radio on and made myself a mug of tea. Then I looked in every room, just to satisfy myself that all was well, closing every door carefully behind me. It's something I always do when I'm in the house alone.

I had a shower, then went into my bedroom. I sat up in bed for a while, thinking of nothing in particular. I switched the radio off but left a light on beside my bed. Yet as soon as I closed my eyes, I couldn't help noticing how loudly my clock was ticking. I never realised my clock was so noisy before. There was no way I could sleep through that.

I got up and stuffed it in the drawer. I snuggled down in bed again. Suddenly, I felt really tired and soon I was drifting off to sleep. So, I was neither awake nor asleep when I first heard it.

Something was tapping against my window. It must be a tree. That's what it was, the branches of a tree. Only there are no trees outside my window. That thought catapulted me awake. I lay listening to the sound again. The tapping was quite light but insistent, as if something out there was wanting to be let in.

I clasped my arms around me. What was it? What the hell was doing that? I should get up, pull the curtains away and see what it is. Years ago, when I was about four and had measles, I heard a sound outside my window. I got out of bed – it was in the afternoon and so my curtains weren't drawn – and saw this massive face looming in at me. I really thought I would explode with fear. Of course, it had only been the window-cleaner. But for weeks afterwards, that big face haunted me. Maybe that was what I was scared of now: of opening the curtains and seeing another face splayed against the glass: the Spirit of Death. I must stop calling it 'the Spirit of Death'. It's just a name but one that really scares me. And once you start scaring yourself, it's like a trap closing around you. Until finally, all you can see is your own fear.

It's much better when I think of the spirit as 'my monster'. That made me think of the abominable snowman and werewolves . . . quite cosy images compared with the Spirit of Death.

But the tapping noise outside was as loud as ever. I buried my head under the pillow. But I could still hear it. In fact, it sounded louder under my pillow.

Then, all at once, the tapping stopped. I strained my ears. No, whatever was out there had gone away. Now I was doing it again. There hadn't been an 'it' out there. I'd created that noise. But how? Maybe it wasn't me. Well, then there'd be a perfectly rational explanation for the tapping noise. And in the morning I'd think of it.

But now everything familiar had slipped away so there was nothing to hang on to. Anything was possible. And then the tapping noise started again.

This time I scrambled out of bed and picked up a coat-hanger which was lying on the floor. I needed to have something in my hand. Then I switched the light off, went over to the window and pulled back the curtains. I stood staring into the darkness, my hands tightening on the coat-hanger. Nothing. There was nothing out there. Slowly, my breathing relaxed. I was pulling the curtains shut again when I felt a rush of icy air brush against my shoulder.

I don't actually remember running out of my bedroom or crashing downstairs. I just remember huddling on the settee, with the television blaring away and the lounge blindingly full of light. I kept thinking of myself staring out of my bedroom window feeling I was safe, when all the time it was there, right beside me, ready to rise up out of the darkness whenever it wanted.

I drowned the lounge with light and noise. But even then, I wasn't safe.

I lay awake until daylight flooded the room.

CHAPTER 6

'THIS WASN'T MY BEDROOM ANY MORE'

I awoke to a strange, far away sound. Then I realised it was the phone. I raced downstairs. It was Mum. I immediately asked how Nan was, although I dreaded the reply. I knew it wouldn't be good news.

'Nan isn't too well at the moment,' said Mum, her voice sounding very thick. 'But she's a fighter, your nan.' How often had we chanted this. Yes, Nan was a fighter and now she was having the fight of her life to hold on to her eighty-seven years.

I said, 'Tell Nan . . .' What could I tell her? Please stay alive? 'Tell Nan, I'm thinking about her.'

'She knows that,' said Mum. 'She did so enjoy seeing you and Louise yesterday. She's talked about nothing else since.' Then Mum started going on about what food there was in the freezer.

I put the phone down and two seconds later it rang again. I assumed it would be Mum with some extra message but instead, it was Geoff Mallender, who ran the local football team I used to play for on Saturdays. They had a match this morning and were a player short – could I stand in?

'You must be desperate,' I joked. But suddenly, playing 'footie' seemed really appealing. For a few hours I could escape from everything.

I didn't play especially well (understatement) but it was just so good to be away. Out there on the football pitch I felt strong and confident.

After the match I lingered for as long as I could. I didn't want to go home. And as soon as I opened the front door I shivered, without knowing why. Maybe it was the silence. All at once I felt very alone. If only Louise were here.

And then I saw the red light of the answer-phone flashing frantically and there was her voice: 'It's only Louise. I just rang to say, "Hi" and why aren't you in, because I hate talking on these things. Anyway, this afternoon my mum's visiting a friend who lives very near you. So I could come over, that's if you're in and not doing anything else, of course. Take care. Bye.'

I rang Louise right away. She'd be over in about an hour. That gave me just enough time to have a shower and make myself look halfway decent.

Louise seemed different this afternoon. For a start, she was a lot paler.

'Are you . . . okay?' I asked.

'Yes, I'm fine,' she said. But I didn't alto-gether believe her. I wished she'd tell me, confide in me.

'I'm upstairs at the moment,' I said.

She followed me upstairs. I opened my bed-room door and then gasped in horror. The room was freezing cold. Immediately I told myself to be rational about this. It was the end of October and rooms can get cold very quickly.

'I'll just go and blast the heating up and get us some coffee. I won't be a minute. Make yourself at home, even though you're not.'

I raced downstairs, switched the heating up as high as it would go, made two coffees – filling the mugs right up to the brim as usual – then went back upstairs. Louise was hunched forward on my white canvas chair, my director's chair.

'It will soon warm up now,' I said. She looked up at me and smiled. I went over to the little table beside her and found just enough space to put the two mugs down.

'Sorry about all the junk in here,' I said, sweeping all the magazines on to the floor, then noticing that I'd thrown Ben's pad on to the floor as well. Immediately, I felt embarrassed. 'I never put things away,' I said. 'That's why this room is such a mess,' and proceeded to balance Ben's pad on top of my college bag. I looked across at Louise, but she didn't appear to have noticed. Instead, she pointed at the guitar resting beside my wardrobe.

'So this is your guitar – and with a mahogany back as well. Play me something, then, Mr Music Man.'

'You don't want to hear me play the guitar,' I said. 'I'll put a tape on, instead. Any requests?'

'Yes, you playing the guitar.'

I gave a short laugh. 'Later,' I said.

'But I can picture you playing the guitar,' she said.

'Yeah, in some grotty wine bar on a Thursday night.' I went over to the tape deck. It was still freezing in here, but it would warm up soon. Give it a few more minutes.

'So how many tapes have you got?' asked Louise.

'About two hundred. I can pull out a tape for every mood. I couldn't get through the day without listening to music – music I want to hear. If I'm in my bedroom, music has got to be on and when I'm eating my dinner, and . . . and . . .' I stared at her. 'You're frozen. Let's go back downstairs.'

'No, I'll warm up in a minute,' she said. I got up, retrieved my dressing-gown from under the bed and put it around her.

'I don't need this,' she said.

'Yes, you do.'

'Now I feel like a little old lady.'

'Just be grateful you don't look like one,' I replied, sitting down opposite her again. 'So what do you think of my bedroom, then, apart from the fact it's very cold?'

She smiled. 'You're terribly insecure about your room, aren't you?'

'No.'

'Yes, you are. Well, I really do like it, especially all your posters.'

'They're to cover up my really boring wall-paper.'

'And I love your lamp. It looks like a flying saucer.'

'Usually I hate lampshades, but this one's an exception. It's so weird.'

'I'm not so sure about your black sheets.' Louise gave me a mischievous smile. 'Don't you find them just a bit depressing?'

'Black's my favourite colour.' Then I stopped. I had this horrible feeling: have you ever been out walking at night and suddenly been convinced that someone was right behind you? You don't hear anyone, it's just a feeling you've got, that someone is so close behind you, you can smell their breath. Well that's exactly what I felt then.

And the sensation was so strong that I had to turn round, just to reassure myself. Instead, the feeling grew stronger than ever.

Meanwhile, Louise was looking at me expectantly. I rambled on, 'So no, I don't find dark sheets depressing. After all, it's a dark world.' I stopped. What made me say that? I didn't know. And I could hardly even hear what Louise was saying now.

For something was hovering in the air, just above me. I could feel it pressing down. I couldn't see it, but it was there, somehow suspended over my head.

Panic shot through me. And a kind of horrible despair, too. This spirit, or monster, or whatever I'd brought back with me, was in control all the time now. Even by day, this wasn't my bedroom any more.

Now I could feel it pressing down even harder. I started shivering. This was like those nightmares when you know something bad is reaching out for you but you can't move. I shot to my feet.

'We've got to get out of here,' I gasped. I reached out my hand to Louise.

She got up, took my hand, then said quietly, 'There's something in this room, isn't there?' I could only gaze at her as she went on. 'As soon as I came in, I felt it, it was like some kind of force. Only I couldn't see it. So I thought it was just inside my head.'

'No, it's inside my head too,' I said, clasping her hand tightly.

'But what is it?'

'I don't know, exactly,' I said. I started pacing about furiously until I caught sight of myself in the mirror. And it was then I saw there was something else in the mirror with me: a dark figure, sitting on my bed. Then, almost before I realised it, the figure had gone. I stared around wildly. 'Did you see something?' I gasped.

'What?' asked Louise.

'Something was sitting on my bed. I saw it in the mirror.'

Louise grabbed my hand. 'Go,' she said. And there was no mistaking the urgency in her voice.

But then I cried out. 'This is my room. This is my room,' I repeated, only now, my voice was starting to crack. 'And I don't want you here, whatever you are.' I turned again to Louise, who started to half-push me towards the door.

We stumbled down the stairs, then we both stopped.

'What was that?' I cried, looking back at my bedroom.

'I don't know,' said Louise. 'It sounded like

something was being thrown about.' And then the sound came again, even louder than before.

'What's it doing in there?' I cried. I made as if to go back.

'No, don't go back,' said Louise, gripping my hand tightly now. Then she asked, 'Do you know what it is?'

I stood silent for a moment. 'Yes, I know what it is,' I said, 'it's the monster I created.'

'Monster?' echoed Louise.

'Yes. I mean it hasn't got the staring, purple eyes I gave it, but otherwise . . .'

'So, it's your monster,' murmured Louise. She sounded almost relieved.

'It's just in my head but somehow you've picked it up too.' I stared at her. 'Look, what am I doing putting you through all this? I'll drop you off home.'

'Don't you dare – in fact – don't even think about it.' Louise sounded so indignant, I even smiled.

She said, 'I saw the monster, or felt it anyway. So I want to help you fight it.'

I stared upstairs. 'This is mad. It didn't exist until I made it exist. And now there's just no way I can control it . . . it's taking me over. Even in the day, now.'

Louise looked into my eyes, then she whispered, 'If you created it, you can destroy it.'

'But can I?' I asked.

She clutched my hand. 'Yes, you've got to fight it, exorcise it.'

'Exorcise it.' The idea took hold. 'Cast it out, you mean?'

'Yes – and only you can do that. Will it still be upstairs?'

'Probably. It's never far away from me.'

'So let's go back upstairs,' she said. 'You can exorcise it. I know you can. Then it will all be over – for you.'

CHAPTER 7

'I DON'T WANT TO GO OUT WITH ANYONE'

As we went upstairs, from far away, came the dull rumble of thunder.

'That's all we need,' murmured Louise. 'Great flashes of lightning as we go into your room.' For the first time she sounded nervous.

'Thunder and lightning's all right,' I said. 'They're part of nature . . . it's this stuff.' I nodded at my bedroom door. Then I lowered my head and charged forward as if I were about to do a rugby tackle. Suddenly, going into my room was like going into enemy territory.

We stood in the doorway together, shivering slightly. The room was deathly cold. The books I'd put on top of my bag were scattered across the floor now. So was Ben's pad. Anger flared up in me. This was my own private room; I'd even trained my parents to knock before they came in. Yet something had been in here, hurling about my belongings. Something to which I had given life.

Louise went over and put Ben's pad back on top of my college bag.

'It had no right touching that – or anything in here,' I cried. Then I hesitated. I'd seen exorcisms on films, of course. But they were exorcising real spirits. Or were they? Maybe that was all in people's heads too.

Anyway, I was finally getting rid of this monster I'd created, my Spirit of Death. Then I cried, 'Be gone from here, haunt me no more. I created you. Now I am casting you out for ever.' I stopped, but my voice still seemed to be echoing around the room. Then there was an intense silence. The room seemed suddenly very still.

'I think it's getting warmer in here,' whispered Louise.

'Yes, I think it is,' I replied. I was almost afraid to agree with her, just in case . . . well, just in case. I sat down on the edge of my bed. This time I couldn't sense anything around me.

'Even the air feels lighter,' said Louise.

'Yes, it does,' I cried, and all at once we were hugging each other delightedly. But I still stared around me, disbelievingly. It left so easily, too easily.

As if reading my thoughts, Louise said, 'We must believe it has gone. If we don't, if our minds are still open to it, then it could still sneak back. But it won't.'

'No, I won't let it.' I stared at her. 'My imagination has become my enemy. But not any more, now I'll tame it – thank you for believing I could do that. Keep believing in me, will you?' Then I hugged and kissed her. Her body felt so warm against mine. I kept pressing her closer to me.

'Don't leave me,' I whispered. I wouldn't normally say this. But now I felt dizzy with exhilaration, almost as if I were drunk.

'Don't leave me,' I whispered again.

'I'll never leave you,' she cried. Now she was melting into my arms; what made us separate was dissolving away. We belonged together – and right then I'd have done anything for her, given her anything.

Finally, she took my hand and guided me towards the door.

'Are you hungry?' she asked.

'A bit. You?'

'Starving.'

'Okay. Shall I see what I can whip up? Have you any special cravings?'

Louise grinned. 'Now there's a question.'

We walked downstairs, arm in arm, giggling with relief.

I opened the freezer and pulled out a packet of chips.

'Nan used to take me out for a meal sometimes and I never wanted to have a pizza or Chinese food, I just wanted a massive plate of chips. They never did chips at our school, they were always trying to get us to eat salads. So were my parents, but when it was just Nan and me, I'd pile my plate up with chips and empty half a bottle of tomato sauce over them . . . good old Nan.'

'We could have chips now, if you like,' said Louise, 'in honour of your nan.'

'Yeah, okay,' I said. 'And I always had a choc-ice to follow.'

'A two-course meal, wonderful,' said Louise.

'I'll tell you something, Louise,' I said, heaping a pile of chips on to a baking tray. 'No one cooks a better chip than me. I make them really crunchy.'

Twenty minutes later I pulled my tray of chips out of the oven. 'Some of these look pretty burnt, actually,' I said.

'I love them burnt,' said Louise.

'Just like me,' I said. 'So help yourself to anything.' I waved at the tomato sauce, vinegar and salt on the table. Then, Louise took her first mouthful of chips. I watched her anxiously.

'Delicious,' she pronounced.

I beamed. 'You see, there's no end to my talents.' Then I waved a chip in the air and said, 'To my nan.'

'To your nan,' repeated Louise.

The chips were an undoubted success, the choc-ices were a different matter. Louise bit into her choc-ice and made a face.

'Oh!' she cried.

'What?'

'Just taste yours.'

'Why?'

'Well, mine tastes of onions.'

'Onions,' I exclaimed, then I took a bite. 'No, this one doesn't.'

'Mine does. It's got a definite onion flavour, not that I mind, I've just never had an onion flavoured choc-ice before.'

I got up. 'I'll get you something else.'

'There's no need.'

74

'No, I will, the family honour is at stake now.'

When I returned I said, 'Hold out your hand,' and slipped an onion into it. After that we got a bit silly and it was just such a relief to laugh and mess about again.

Then we went back upstairs to my room. I put on a tape and sat beside Louise on my bed. I put my arm around her and made some silly joke – I can't remember what now – but she laughed. She laughed at most of my jokes.

I was trying so hard to be mellow and relaxed, but I couldn't help noticing how dark my room was getting. I'd seen off my monster in the afternoon. But it was now when it could suddenly burst out of my imagination again. My imagination and the dark: what a powerful combination that was. Could I ever really defeat them?

As if reading my thoughts Louise said, 'You've won, you know, you really have. Your monster has gone for ever.'

'You reckon?'

'Yes, your monster has gone. You've got to believe that.' She sounded so fervent, I looked at her and smiled.

Then I said, 'I've just discovered something about you . . . at night, your eyes get greener.'

She looked up at me, amused, intrigued. 'No, they don't . . . you're making that up.'

'I'm not.' I gave a half-laugh. 'But I wouldn't trust anything I say, I mean, seventeen years old and I'm talking about seeing monsters. My monster.' I nodded my head contemptuously. 'Every time I say that I think of Frankenstein hiding in my wardrobe or something. That helps. But it's not really like a monster.'

Louise looked up. 'What's it like?'

'It's more of a spirit, a dark spirit, darker than the blackest sky.' I stopped. For Louise was staring at me now. And in her eyes I saw terror.

Then it was gone. It was like a snapshot. But I had seen it. I took hold of her hand. 'First I spook Danny up with my stupid story . . . now you.'

'No, you didn't, not really,' she said slowly. 'Tell me more about it.'

'It's got purple eyes. When I made it up, it had anyway. I've never seen them in real life . . . Real life, now there's an interesting phrase. What exactly is real life?'

My tone was more than a bit flippant but Louise didn't seem to pick that up. Instead, she was staring at me, intently.

'Where did you first see this dark spirit?'

'At Abbotts Hill. Like I said. I made up the spirit to scare Danny and then I saw it there – or I thought I did. It was after we'd seen that red light and Danny and Angie had run to the car. I saw it there in the church, just for a second.'

Louise let out a gasp.

'Look, what are we talking about this for?' I began.

'No, no, it's interesting,' she said. 'And where else did you see it?'

'Well, it's followed me around. I've sensed it in my bedroom and I saw it . . .'

'In Ben's room, that night,' she interrupted.

'Yes, that's right.'

'What exactly did you see?'

'I saw this black shape rush across the room. It happened very fast. I told your mum. I think she thought I'd had a nightmare.'

'That's what she told me,' said Louise.

'Because you had a nightmare too, didn't you?' I said.

Louise didn't answer this. Instead, she got up and went over to my mirror. 'And you saw it through the mirror. What a thing to see staring at you.'

I got up too. Her green eyes looked suddenly huge, but the rest of her face seemed drawn in, making it look very long and pinched. I took her in my arms. 'What does it matter what I saw. It was just in my imagination and it's all over now. You told me that.'

'Yes, that's right.' She gave a rather dazed smile. My arms were close around her now.

'I should be a horror writer,' I said. 'My tales really seem to scare people.'

'Yes, maybe you should.'

'Imagination is an amazing thing, isn't it?' I said.

She murmured her agreement.

'Not that I shall be thinking that at two in the morning.'

Then I looked at Louise. Probably all that's happened today has been a real ordeal for her. Yet she'd suffered it for me. 'You know, you've been pretty heroic today,' I said. She smiled.

'No, you have, you've really helped me.'

'I'm glad', she said, softly, but then she turned away. Was I embarrassing her with my praise – well, she deserved it.

'I don't flash compliments around, you know . . . I couldn't have got through all this without you.'

I waited for her to turn round again. But she didn't. Instead, there was a moment of silence before she said, 'But that's what friends are for.' Then she went and sat down on the bed again. She looked suddenly far away. But I couldn't see her very clearly, I was too busy listening to a word crashing about in my head.

Friends. The word was colliding everywhere. FRIENDS.

We're much more than friends. But she said we were just friends.

I got up. 'I'll put on another tape,' I announced. I had to do something, if only to quieten down all these voices in my head. Yet somehow they screamed over the music.

'Friends – you and Louise are just friends.'

'No, she didn't exactly say that,' I tried to scream back.

So what had she said then?

Suddenly she was asking me a question. 'What are we listening to now, Rich?'

I hadn't even looked. 'A surprise.'

I sat down heavily beside her. 'Louise . . .' I hesitated. Then I gave a sick little laugh, before asking, 'Are we meant to be going out together?'

She looked astonished, as if this had come right out of the blue. Then it was her turn to release the sick laugh, before saying, 'Well I'm very flattered and I do like you a lot . . .' She went gabbling on, saying all these flattering things about me, but

I wasn't listening because I could hear something else vibrating down the track. And then it came thundering towards me, a truly massive, 'But I don't think I want to get into a relationship with anyone right now.'

My face was tightening so fast I could barely croak, 'Why?'

'Oh, well,' she squirmed awkwardly. 'It's just, the last person I went out with I knew as a friend first. And when we were just good friends we got on so well together. Then, as soon as we started going out together, it changed both of us. I know I became so picky, all his funny little habits started annoying me when I hadn't even noticed them before . . .'

She paused, looking at me for some kind of support, but I kept my face blank. I just thought, why compare me to him?

She went on. 'Then I'll be thinking I've got to ring you every day and all the spontaneity just goes. So please, for now, can we just be friends, really good friends?' She looked at me, almost pleadingly.

It was then I noticed what tape was playing; it was a Smiths' song, *Asleep*. And I thought, I'll never be able to listen to that song again. But I just said, 'Yeah' and raised my eyebrows.

'I don't think I've said this very well.' Louise gave a nervous smile. 'I feel awful now.' I gave her a very bleak stare. She has just knocked me to the ground and now she wants my sympathy. 'I do think a lot of you,' she said, her voice warm, coaxing.

But inside me all the voices were laughing now: ugly, twisted laughs. 'I do think such a lot of you,' that was offered up to me as an afterthought, a PS to my letter of rejection. She was saying some other stuff now. But I'd stopped listening. Instead, I heard that voice inside my head, saying, 'Girls: you really mess up with girls. Your last girlfriend was seeing someone else for two months and you never even realised . . . not for a moment. Now this time you misread it again. She doesn't want to go out with you. Not in a million years.'

I got up. I felt so humiliated I didn't think I could bear to stay in the same room as her. 'Can we just be good friends?' Those are words you should never say to anyone. 'I don't fancy you' is a lot fairer. That was what she was really saying. So why couldn't she at least be honest about it?

And all that stuff she said about not wanting to go out with anyone. That was just waffle, wasn't it? When the right guy came along, she'd be there with him.

But she didn't fancy me. So in that case, what was she doing ringing me up every day, spending all this time with me, kissing me and . . . what was going on? She was crazy. She'd put all the groundwork in; we were building up this amazing relationship. And now, she'd just thrown it all away. There was nothing left. We had nowhere to go. We were just stuck in limbo now.

Still, I had one consolation; if I hadn't asked her about us today I'd still be seeing her every day, putting all that effort in, believing . . . at least now I knew.

It was then I dredged up something Angie had told me. She said that when Scott Flynn had gone out with Louise he'd finished with her because Louise played her cards too close to her chest.

I hated Scott Flynn. Yet, right then, I felt an unexpected flash of solidarity with him. He was right. That's what made Louise such a very frustrating person to be around. She was too mysterious. You never felt you got the real her.

'Are you all right?' She was staring at me, her eyes lost in shadow.

'I'm okay.'

'It's just, you've gone very quiet.'

I shrugged my shoulders. 'Let's go downstairs, shall we?'

She looked slightly surprised at this. But what was the point of being up here now? We're finished.

Downstairs I made her a coffee and she started trying to make jokes about the chips. But I couldn't join in. I couldn't really hear her, to be honest, I was tuned into a different frequency and all they played was, 'Can we just be friends?'

Round and round the words went. No wonder I felt so giddy. I almost hated her. Actually, I think I did hate her, as much as I hated myself for being so gullible. And then she gave me one of her sad, little smiles and I felt such a rush of longing for her I had to look away.

I just wanted her to go home. But instead, we sat downstairs with the television droning on and the rain smashing itself against the windows until finally she said, 'I suppose I'd better go.'

'I'll give you a lift,' I said.

'Are you sure? I can always ring up Mum.'

'There's no need for that.' I looked outside. 'It's chucking it down now. You're going to get soaked just walking to the car.' I handed her my umbrella.

'What about you?' she asked.

'I'm all right,' I muttered. What did I care about getting wet now? I didn't even run to the car. I just let the rain sweep into my face. As we drove along, lightning suddenly lit the car up, followed by the crashing of thunder.

'That's getting a bit too close,' exclaimed Louise.

'I like thunder,' I announced.

'Not at night, though.'

'Yeah, it's brilliant, best time. Everything going really dark and the birds getting all chirpy just before it starts. And all that power building up and then just ripping the whole world apart . . . love it. Love it.' Louise gave me a puzzled look but she didn't reply. We didn't say much for the rest of the journey. Every so often the lightning flashed through the car like a giant spotlight, but we both just stared ahead. She was slipping further and further away from me now.

We reached her house. 'Thanks for all your help today,' I said, but my tone was cool and formal. I picked the umbrella up. 'You'll need this.'

She hesitated, then she attempted a small smile. 'But you like the rain, don't you?' She took the umbrella from me and then put her hand on top of mine. She squeezed my hand quite hard, looking straight at me. But I just gave her a grim stare.

Why should I make it easy for her? She'd cheated me – us – out of so much.

'Rich, make sure you keep in contact, won't you?' she said. 'See you soon.' She squeezed my hand again.

She was being really nice to me. But I knew why. It was so she wouldn't feel guilty; I saw through those warm gestures and buried them. I said, 'I'll see you around.' To all the people I never see again, my last words always are, 'I'll see you around.' What I'm really saying, is, I don't want to make any arrangements to see you. If I bump into you, fine, otherwise, forget it.

Louise was out of the car now. I heard her say, 'Bye then,' very softly and then she ran into the house.

I drove away. I'd really cut her down, hadn't I? I was triumphant for all of two seconds. Then I began to regret it, drastically.

CHAPTER 8

'PLEASE LET ME IN'

The phone was ringing impatiently when I opened the door. It must be Louise. It has to be Louise. Please God let it be Louise. How I raced to that phone, I even beat the answer-phone.

It was my mum.

'Have you just got in?' she asked.

I was so breathless with disappointment I could hardly speak. 'That's right,' I panted. 'Just taken Louise back. When are you home, then?'

'That's why I've rung. We can't come home tonight as we'd hoped, because Uncle David's been delayed and we can't leave your nan on her own, especially as . . . you know how much she hates thunder.'

I certainly did. Years ago now, I was staying with Nan when there was this mighty thunderstorm. And right away, Nan was throwing everything out of the cupboard under the stairs: the Hoover, everything and then she'd go and sit in the cupboard until the storm was over. She made me go in with her, too.

I tried arguing with her about it. I gave a little

smile as I saw my seven-year-old self earnestly trying to explain to Nan that there was nothing to be afraid of. She didn't believe me, of course. Poor Nan. How she must hate having to stay in her bedroom tonight. Or maybe she doesn't care any more. I remembered when I had measles really badly, all the things that had been bothering me just fell away. I hoped it was the same for Nan.

'How is Nan?' I asked.

A tiny pause. I could almost hear Mum taking a deep breath. 'We're all keeping our fingers crossed.' Another meaningless sentence. Today has been littered with them.

Then Mum changed the subject. 'Did you find the food in the freezer all right?'

'Oh yeah, fine.' Somehow that meal with Louise seemed weeks away now.

'So you're not starving then,' said Mum. 'I hope the thunder doesn't keep you awake. See you soon. Take care.'

It was a blow Mum and Dad not coming home tonight. I didn't particularly want to talk to them or anything, I just wanted to know they were around. Still, it was late and I felt really tired. So with any luck I'd be asleep in a few minutes. I didn't want to lie awake thinking about Louise or dark spirits. I just wanted sweet oblivion.

I fell into bed. Then, despite all my plans, I lay there for what must have been hours, just thinking about Louise. Somehow I couldn't push her away.

I was glad about one thing: that she'd taken my umbrella. Maybe some time she'll look at that umbrella and feel guilty. Maybe. But anyway, that umbrella will remind her of me. That was good, for I wanted to be remembered, even though I doubted if I'd ever see her again. I knew I'd probably come across her at college, where we'd exchange embarrassed 'Hellos' but that would be all. It was over (not that it had ever really started for Louise). And yet, how many more nights will I spend lying awake for hours, just thinking about her?

Months after I broke up with my last girlfriend, I'd still be going over things she'd said and missing her, without quite knowing why. So how long before I can say 'Goodbye' to Louise, my nearly girlfriend. Place your bets please: what do you give me, six months . . . a year . . . ten years . . . After that cheerful thought, I fell asleep almost at once.

I was awoken by a voice. My voice.

I was saying, 'There's no one here at the moment, so please leave your message after the beep and thanks for calling.'

I shot up in bed. The phone must have been ringing. I leaned forward to listen to the message but all I could hear were the beeps and then nothing. Had someone rung off? Louise?

I looked at my watch. But she wouldn't ring at half-past two in the morning, would she? Unless she was missing me so much she couldn't help herself. This was such a bewitching idea I spun it out a little more. She'd been lying awake for hours, then on impulse, she rushed downstairs, desperate to talk to me, but instead she'd got the answer-phone. And she couldn't speak her message of love to me on a machine.

But then I thought maybe it was Mum ringing to tell me that Nan . . . No, I couldn't imagine Mum ringing me in the middle of the night like that.

So who was it? A madman who was downstairs impersonating my voice, hoping to lure me into the lounge where he could stab me? I managed to smile at that idea, eventually.

But I didn't want to be awake now. This wasn't my time. Yet I couldn't sleep either, not while I kept asking myself who had rung me up.

It must be Louise. Maybe she was sitting by her phone wondering if she dared ring me again.

'Go on Louise, do it,' I urged her, aloud. Of course it was her. If only I hadn't been asleep.

Then, all at once, my whole room was flooded with light. For a second my room was safe. But then the light died away and there was a great roar of thunder and nothing but darkness again. While downstairs, I was saying, 'There's no one here at the moment, so please leave your message after the beep and thanks for calling.' Then came the beeps and a deep mournful silence as I realised, with a thud of disappointment, what had happened: The thunder was causing little power cuts which were setting the answer-phone off.

All at once I felt irrationally angry with Louise. Why hadn't she rung? Because she didn't care, that way why. She was probably fast asleep now, while I was tossing and turning like this.

But then I remembered how pale and tired she'd looked today. And what about the night I'd seen her walking up the stairs in that strange kind of trance.

Louise was awake now. I was certain of it. Or rather, something was keeping her awake. Well, it wasn't me. That thought hardened my heart; this wasn't the time to start feeling sorry for Louise.

And then it happened again.

A great burst of light and, instantaneously this time, darkness and an outbreak of thunder which seemed to make the whole house shake.

I sat up in bed clutching the blankets around me. While, from downstairs, 'There's no one here at the moment, so please leave your message after the beep and thanks for calling.'

That was still my voice, wasn't it? Only I sounded different this time, older, somehow. What gibberish. Yet, the way that voice kept repeating, 'There's no one here at the moment,' made me feel quite weird. It was as if in some way I'd stopped existing. That was gibberish too. But right now, I really don't want to hear myself say that any more.

I decided to go downstairs and unplug the answer-phone. I got out of bed and groped my way downstairs. Then I opened the lounge door. My head felt fuzzy and it was quite cold now. Outside I could hear the rain drumming against the windows. I stood, listening to it for a moment, then reached out for the phone.

As I did so, it let out one short ring. I sprang back, waiting for the phone to ring again. But it didn't. Now what was going on? Suddenly, and without knowing why, I picked the phone up.

I didn't hear the dialling tone as I'd expected. Instead there was all this crackling. There must be water on the line, but how odd it sounded. The crackling just went on and on too. I was about to put the phone down when I heard someone talking. The voice sounded far away. Well, it was probably hundreds of miles away. Somehow, the phone had picked up this call. It has done that before.

Then I heard the voice again. Only it was much clearer this time. It was a child's voice. A boy.

'Hello.'

I remember thinking what a strange time for a boy to be phoning anyone.

'Hello,' repeated the boy. His voice was suddenly amazingly clear.

'Hello,' I said, without really expecting the boy to hear me.

There was a pause, when all I could hear was more crackling but then the voice came through, as clearly as before. 'Let me in. Please let me in,' it said.

That voice was talking to me. But how could it be? 'Who is this?' I demanded.

'Let me in,' the voice repeated. 'Please let me in.'

'What is this, some kind of sick joke?' I cried and flung the phone down.

Then I stood there taking deep breaths to try and steady myself. It was the shock of the phone ringing like that and then hearing that child's voice on the other end. It was obviously someone messing around. But he sounded so young – and so desperate. No wonder it shook me up.

I then noticed how hushed and quiet everything seemed. I couldn't even hear the rain any more. Everything had stopped, except for my brain. That was racing ahead trying to find a logical explanation. But there wasn't one.

I gazed around me. Everything was real and yet nothing felt real. I was in some strange middle world, where I'd just been talking to . . . what exactly?

Then, suddenly, nothing could stop me shaking.

CHAPTER 9

'IT'S TIME FOR YOU TO MOVE ON'

Early next morning I was banging on Danny's door. His mum answered. She saw right away something was wrong. I must have looked awful. I'd hardly slept all night. I heard her rush upstairs to Danny and say, 'Richard's downstairs looking very upset.'

She came back down and insisted on giving me tea and toast before leaving for work. Then Danny appeared, yawning madly. He grinned at me slumped on his sofa. 'You look totally wrecked,' he said.

'Thanks.'

'Something happened between you and Louise then?'

I repeated her name to myself. A pain stabbed my heart.

'Not exactly. In a way, yes.'

Danny thumped down beside me. 'Sort your life out, Richard.' He was still grinning but he spoke quite gently – for Danny.

Then I told Danny everything: from me first seeing the spirit at Abbotts Hill, right up to last night's ghostly phone call. I could hear myself narrating the events in this really flat, weary voice. Maybe that was why Danny didn't interrupt me once.

When I was finished he just sat staring at me, before declaring, 'I can't think when I'm hungry.'

So he made us both bacon and egg. Strangely enough, I felt hungry too. We sat round the kitchen table with Radio One blaring away. Then I asked, 'So what do you think happened last night?'

Danny hesitated for a moment, then said, 'I think you got yourself in a right state about Louise and her not wanting to go out with you.'

'Well . . .'

'Come on, you did. I know you.'

'All right.'

'So then,' continued Danny, 'you were on your own, the phone goes in the middle of the night and your imagination takes over.'

'But a voice.'

'If you can conjure up dark spirits all over the place, a voice should be no problem.' Danny leant back in his chair. 'I'm still hungry. Do you want any more toast, Rich?'

'Go on then.'

Danny got up, put some bread in the toaster then sat down again. 'Okay, let's just say you really did hear a voice,' he said. 'It was a little kid's voice, wasn't it?'

'Yes.'

'Then it has to be, what's his name, Ben, Louise's brother.'

'But why?'

'Well, Ben asked you to let him in, so he obviously can't get into your house without help.'

'But why does Ben want to get into my house?'

'You've got me there,' said Danny.

Then Danny's phone rang and he disappeared for ages while I sat chewing my way through a couple more rounds of toast. All of a sudden, I couldn't stop eating.

When he came back he said, 'That was Angie. We're supposed to be going out this morning. I've put her off.'

'Thanks.' I was more grateful than I sounded. Since he'd gone out with Angie I hardly ever saw him on his own. It was as if they didn't exist as separate people any more. And, much as I like Angie, I resented that.

'I've been thinking,' he went on. 'I reckon we need help from the professionals.'

'Call in the ghostbusters, you mean?'

'Something like that. I was thinking of Harry, up the road.'

'Harry, the medium.' I'd always just seen him as a bad joke.

'He's helped quite a lot of people,' said Danny. I looked doubtful. Danny went on. 'It's not going to do any harm, is it?'

'All right,' I said quietly. I needed rescuing and I couldn't be too choosy about who did it.

So Danny arranged for us to go over to Harry's for two o'clock. Before that, we ate even more food and then, as two o'clock drew nearer, we started getting really silly. In the end we were laughing hysterically at everything.

'Look, we can't go to Harry's like this. Come on, let's get rid of all our laughing now,' said Danny.

But we were still laughing as we set off to Harry's house. I even started doing an impression of Harry. In a quavery voice I said, 'And after I saw the spirits it just changed my life and I never wore green underpants again.'

'He's not like that,' began Danny.

And that was when I saw Harry, standing in his doorway, obviously waiting for us. He was older and smaller than I'd expected but tanned and dapper with long white sideburns. His brown eyes looked shrewd and alert. He was wearing a casual grey jersey, but underneath the jersey was a white shirt and a large yellow cravat.

After Danny had introduced us, Harry smiled and nodded, then said to me, 'You don't think I'm a prat, do you?'

That gave me a shock, I can tell you. I felt as if he'd just looked right inside my head. 'No, of course not,' I muttered.

'Good.' Harry smiled. 'I always ask that question. You see, I'm just an ordinary person. I don't do any magic or hocus-pocus.' He smiled again, as if he had said something funny. 'So come through. I thought we'd be best in the study.' We followed him through the lounge and into a much smaller room, lined with old paperbacks.

'Sit down. Make yourself at home,' said Harry. 'But not there, Richard.' I started. Was a spirit reclining in that particular chair? But then he said, 'The dog sits there, so it's full of hairs.'

So I squashed beside Danny on the small tweed settee, while Harry leant back in the matching tweed chair. He looked very relaxed. The wall behind him was covered in photographs. In the centre of the pictures was a large photograph of a girl, whom I assumed was his daughter, in a cap and gown.

'There are various things I can tell you,' said Harry. He crossed his legs and I could see the bunions peeping out of his slip-on shoes. 'But, like I told you, there's nothing special about me. The spirits come through me, that's all. I'm only a channel.'

Harry went on. 'I've seen the spirits since I was about four or five. I saw these little children in my garden and would play with them for hours. We had some wonderful games. But no one else could see them. My dear mother thought I just had some imaginary friends. They weren't imaginary but they were my friends – and have been my friends ever since. When I was sixteen, they even saved my life.' He paused dramatically. 'One afternoon, I was on my own and just about to cross the road when I felt these hands grab me. I couldn't see anything but I felt them all right, very strong they were.' He gave a little chuckle. 'I didn't know what was going on until out of nowhere this lorry appeared, roaring along at a great old speed. I'd been saved from certain death.'

I stared at him doubtfully. Then I thought, if the spirit people could save lives, why didn't they save Ben? As if reading my thoughts, Harry said, 'I can't explain everything but I can tell you this. We think we're masters of our own destiny, but we're not. We all have some role to play. It may only be a brief one. But then you can't measure the significance of a life by how long it is. It's how you've live it and what impact you made on . . .'

The door opened and a tiny silver-haired woman appeared, wheeling a tea trolley. She put the trolley beside Harry. She was wearing a black jumper and trousers, and had a bit of a limp.

'I thought you'd like some tea,' she said. We made polite murmuring noises and she chatted briefly with Danny, asking about his mum, all that stuff. Then she said, 'I've locked Lucy in the kitchen.' Noticing my rather startled look she said, 'Lucy's our dog and when there's food about she won't give you any peace.' She handed around cups of tea, said, 'Help yourself to sugar,' and put down a plate of biscuits. The biscuits looked distinctly crumbly and old. I wondered how long they'd been on the plate. Maybe they were glued on. Neither Danny nor I touched them – nor did Harry, actually. She looked across at her husband. 'Don't let him go on too long, will you. He'll talk all day if you let him.' She gave a sly smile. 'Never believed in any of it, myself.'

'You can't make anyone believe,' said her husband, good-humouredly.

'He does healing too, you know,' said his wife. 'Yet he's never been able to heal this.' She pointed to her left leg.

He shook his head. 'Sometimes I can tune into the power, sometimes I can't.'

She gave another little smile just as if she were humouring him, letting him have his little delusion. And yet he didn't look like a man who was easily fooled.

As soon as his wife had gone I leant forward. 'Danny has told you what's happened to me.'

He raised a chunky hand. 'I'm coming to that.'

But I couldn't wait any longer. 'What do you think it all means? Like the phone call.'

He bristled at my impatience. 'What I've been trying to tell you is that I slowly discovered I had the gift of seeing the spirit people. So now . . . well, it's a bit like a zip-up jacket. You unzip it when you want but you can always zip it back up again, can't you? So it is with those who can see the spirits. I open myself to the power when I want to. But I can close that power off again too. So I control it. Now, you – you may have the gift too. But you've discovered it the wrong way.'

'How do you mean?' I asked.

'You invented this spirit and then you went to Abbotts Hill. Now, what you saw may just have been a physical manifestation of your fear. But what you've got to remember is that there really are spirits all around, calling out to us, sending us signals, trying to make contact. And I think you've somehow opened yourself up to the spirit world. And maybe, maybe, you are also picking up a genuine spirit.' He gave a mirthless chuckle. 'That's the trouble with you people who meddle in things, you don't know what you're picking up. I always say to those who mess about with ouija boards, what kind of spirit is going to hang around a ouija board?'

'So there are bad spirits,' I gasped.

'You enter the next world as you've lived here,' he replied. 'We take all our vices with us. I had a spirit come through recently and the first thing I noticed was his cigar smoke. I could smell it. No, there are bad people in this world and the next.'

'And you think I've picked up a bad spirit?'

'I don't know,' he said. 'At the moment you're very susceptible, so you must be careful.' Then he added, more gently, 'But from what happened last night, I think you've picked up a poor little child crying for attention. They get so frustrated and lonely. Sometimes it takes them a while to realise they're on the spirit side. They throw things around because they don't understand why we're ignoring them.'

'So they can see us, then?' asked Danny. Danny had moved nearer to me on the settee and kept patting me on the shoulder, as much to reassure himself as me, while from next door came the sound of the television. Harry's wife was apparently watching the racing.

'Oh yes, the spirits get very agitated, especially if there's something they want to tell us. I've helped quite a few of them to move on.'

'When they move on, do they grow up?' I asked.

'Some of them grow up, some of them don't,' said Harry. 'But there are schools and universities on the spirit side, you know.'

That was when I stopped believing him. I'd taken in all that stuff about children not knowing they were dead and wanting attention. But when he started talking about schools and universities for them – he was fantasising now, wasn't he, trying to pin this world on to the next.

'I hope they don't have exams as well,' said Danny.

Harry just laughed and said, 'I can tell you, all the children are well and happy in the spirit world. For they are God's special children who don't need to spend much time on earth.'

I had a feeling he had said this many times before. And it was all just so happy and darling and lovely. It was a sweet dream, with all the pain ironed out. But was it anything else? You couldn't be sure of anything, could you? All this talk of spirits could just be more proof of the power of imagination. There was nothing to hold on to.

'And that phone call Rich got,' said Danny. 'Could that really have been from a spirit?'

'Oh yes, there have been a number of cases of people talking to spirits; sometimes they didn't even realise they were talking to a dead person, until afterwards. There are cases going right back to the 1920s.'

So that was all right then! What Harry didn't seem to realise was that not everyone wanted to pick up the phone and start chatting with someone who'd died a year ago.

'I just wanted all this to end,' I said. 'Look, let's say I have opened myself up to this spirit. How can I stop seeing – and hearing – it?'

99

'Very easily,' said Harry. 'Next time you see it, just say, "Leave me now. It's time for you to move on." You need only say this very quietly, very gently.'

'And it will go?' I interrupted.

'If it's a good spirit, it will go at once,' said Harry.

'And if it doesn't?' I asked.

'Then come and see me again,' said Harry.

An hour later Danny and I were back at my house. We'd spent that last hour just driving around, while I went over everything I'd seen. Suddenly, Danny wanted to know all about it.

I put the key in my door. I was walking into my own home. So why did I feel so strange and lost? I looked around warily. Somehow, I was far away from everything I knew. Nothing seemed familiar.

Maybe that's why I ran to the answer-phone. But there was no message from Louise. Why hadn't she rung? There was nothing from my parents either. That was strange. Mum would usually have rung through by now, just to check that I was all right. I could always call her. I knew where she was. But this silence could only mean bad news. And I was scared.

'Can you pick up anything?' asked Danny. Since we'd spoken with Harry, he had a greatly inflated view of my supernatural gifts.

'Something doesn't feel right,' I said. 'But I don't sense any spirits.'

'So what's the first sign of a spirit?' asked Danny.

'Usually it gets very cold, only the cold is inside you. It feels like someone's rubbing an ice-cube up and down your back. But it was only upstairs I ever felt that.'

'Let's go upstairs then,' said Danny. 'You can go first,' he added.

So then we prowled around my bedroom for a few minutes. 'There's nothing here,' I said. Then I put on a tape and we both sat on my bed.

'So do you reckon you'll get another call tonight?' asked Danny.

'I don't know.'

'And if you do, what are you going to say to it?'

'Have you passed your haunting exams yet?'

'And when are you going to university?' laughed Danny. 'No, come on, I mean, this ghost wants to come inside, doesn't it? Will you let it? As you have the gift, brother.'

'The only gift I've got is for scaring myself silly.'

'But if you see anything tonight, you will give me a bell, won't you?' asked Danny.

'Why don't you stay over?' I said. 'I'll even cook you tea, if you like.'

'Yeah, well, I'd really like to,' said Danny. He gave an embarrassed smile. 'It's just, I've got a tour of duty.' That was how he referred to his time with Angie. 'We're supposed to be going to see some film or other . . . don't even know what it is. Come with us.'

'No, that's all right.'

'I'll tell you what,' said Danny. 'If you see anything weird tonight, give me a bell. I'll be at Angie's all night and I'm sure I can sneak out.'

'Okay mate,' I said. 'Thanks.'

I dropped Danny at Angie's house, where she was waiting impatiently. Now Danny was back where he belonged, in her custody. That annoyed me. Yet, I envied Danny like hell, too.

I drove home feeling totally shattered. I was relieved when I finally parked my car in the driveway. It had just gone half-past five, but already the darkness was settling in. I got out of the car and then blinked in amazement.

Someone was standing in my doorway. I rushed forward. A boy was looking into the darkness. I could see his face, his dark hair, his arms and his shoulders, but that was all. He didn't appear to have any lower body. He seemed to just glide there, twisting slightly from side to side like some kind of puppet, while his face was staring right at me. I struggled to think. But I couldn't. I was too busy trying to breathe.

And then the words Harry had instructed me to say were out of my mouth before I realised it.

'Leave me! Leave me. It's time to move on.'

All at once I was just facing darkness again, while around me everything seemed wrapped in silence.

Those words had worked as swiftly as Harry had predicted. In less than a second, that figure had disappeared into the darkness.

Was it Ben?

It hadn't been clear enough to see. Still, it must have been a good spirit. I almost regretted my words now. I'd been too hasty. But it took me by surprise. It unnerved me. Now I'd cast it out. Or had I? Surely a few whispered words wouldn't get rid of it for good?

I'd just opened the front door when I heard the sharp cry of the telephone. Startled, I froze in the doorway. Then the phone let out another cry that sounded even more urgent. I walked slowly over to the phone, then made a grab for it.

'Rich, it's Angie.'

I was more than a bit surprised. 'All right, Angie.'

'Danny told me about you and Louise,' she said. I groaned inwardly. Was I about to get an 'Angie' lecture? 'So I rang her – just to say, hello, and she sounded so strange.'

'How do you mean?'

'I don't know. Just strange. I think there's something wrong . . .' Her words hung in the air for a moment. Then Angie went on. 'And I think you should go round and see her, or at least ring her.'

I ached to see Louise but somehow, I couldn't, not like that. 'Get her to ring me first,' I said.

'Oh Rich, there's no time for all that.'

Angie was right. If Louise did need help, I should be there now. Yet, just as I was thinking this, came such a hot surge of pain, it made my eyes water.

Louise hurt me last night – hurt my stupid pride, I mean. But pride's not important, not really. Or rather, other things matter a hell of a lot more, like love and friendship. Louise was offering me friendship. Just friendship. But friendship can be a hell of a lot. The most. And what kind of friend have I been?

'Rich, are you still there?' asked Angie.

'Yeah, I'm still here,' I said.

'I am worried about her,' said Angie. 'She said something really strange about you too.'

'What?'

'She said she'd messed up your life.'

I was too stunned to respond to this at first.

'Do you know what she's talking about?' said Angie.

'Haven't a clue.' I was trying to keep my voice light. But the words were pounding in my head. Then I said, 'Leave it to me, Angie, I'm going round to Louise's now.'

CHAPTER 10

THE DEAD HOUR

I roared off to Louise's house. Something was badly wrong. I knew it. I should have rung her this morning. Why didn't I? WHY DIDN'T I?

I jumped out of the car and raced up the drive. I rang the doorbell. No one appeared. I was really anxious now. But she must be in. I rang the doorbell again.

And then the door opened – and there was Louise.

Her skin was deathly pale, making her face seem eerily unreal, like a mask. Only her green eyes seemed larger than ever: wide and staring and lost.

'This is a surprise,' she said.

I felt deeply embarrassed. And neither of us was making eye-contact. 'I came to see if you were all right. Angie was worried.'

Her voice tightened. 'I'm fine, as you see. By the way, I've still got your umbrella,' she added. 'I'll get it for you.' And before I could reply, she was gone again.

Last night we were so close. Now when we

meet we push each other further apart. And I'd do anything for Louise, give her anything. Yet, I can't tell her I'm worried about her, I have to rattle on about Angie. I must look as if I'm only here because of Angie.

Louise returned and handed me my umbrella.

'No, keep it,' I said.

She looked surprised. 'It's okay, I've got an umbrella.'

'Well, have two umbrellas. I want you to have it – please.'

A light came into her eyes. 'Are you in a rush?'

'Not at all,' I said.

Now, for the first time we were looking at each other.

'Would you like a coffee?'

Never have I wanted a coffee more in my life. We were smiling at each other now.

'Come on in then,' said Louise, suddenly sounding like her old self again. 'I'm in the kitchen.' She flashed me a smile. 'I'll just put my new umbrella away.'

I walked into the kitchen, when I saw a tray had been set up. 'That's for Mum,' said Louise. 'She's got a nasty cold and I've made her go to bed. Lots of fluids, that's what she needs, that and lots of rest. I'm being very strict with her. She's supposed to be at some meeting – she's always supposed to be at a meeting – but I nagged and nagged her . . .' Louise looked as if she could do with a good rest herself. She was unnaturally pale. Something was wrong.

Then she asked, 'How's your nan?'

'Not so good,' I said, faintly.

'Your nan is so nice,' said Louise. 'I do hope . . .'

'So do I,' I said softly.

Louise took the tray upstairs to her mum, while I drank my coffee in the lounge. I noticed again the total absence of photographs; quite a contrast to Nan's house, and mine, come to that. My mum insists on displaying every deeply embarrassing picture of me she can find. Still, at least it made the room seem more personal. This lounge felt more like a waiting room.

Louise returned. 'Mum said, or rather croaked, "Hello".'

'Hello, Mum,' I said.

Louise sat down opposite me. I hated her sitting so far away. I wanted her beside me. I wanted to hug and hug her. But first I had to say, 'About last night. I'm sorry.'

She shrugged her shoulders.

'No, I do owe you an apology.'

'You just shut me out last night, didn't you?' said Louise. 'And that was so frustrating.' But her tone was gentle, low-key. 'I said something and then your face went bang.' I smiled. 'And then you were looking at the table and I thought, he's not even listening to me. It was like this great iron gate had come down . . .'

'Yes, I do that.'

'You just shut me out,' she repeated, 'and I knew you'd picked it up all wrong. But you had that look in your face and I couldn't get through. You just sat staring at your stereo . . .'

I laughed. Then she laughed too and said, 'Still, I don't think I explained it very well. Not that I can explain it, really. I tell you, you've had a lucky escape, not going out with me.'

I stared at her. 'What does that mean?'

'You really don't want to know.'

'Now, *you're* blocking *me* out,' I said.

'No, I'm not. I just . . .'

'Tell me.'

'Let's just say, it's not you who should be apologising to me.'

'What does that mean?'

She looked away.

'Oh come on, don't half-tell me something like that. It's so annoying.' There was real frustration in my voice now. Each time we seemed close, one of us would pull away again. Neither of us spoke for a moment. Then I said, 'Come on, one annoying person deserves another – tell me.'

Her eyes suddenly looked very dark and very afraid. Then, in a very small voice, she said, 'It's all my fault, what's been happening to you. It's my fault.'

She sank back in her chair and even the light around her seemed to grow pale and bleak.

'What do you mean?' I asked gently. 'Tell me.'

'Will you ever forgive me?' she said. 'But you see, I didn't know . . . until last night.'

'Know what?'

'It's not you that's being haunted, Rich, it's me. For a while now I've been haunted by this dark spirit.' I started and she gave a breathless laugh. 'You see, the dark spirit you've been seeing is

108

mine. I see him mainly at night, in dreams. At first I just saw him from a distance. I'd look out of the window and see him watching me. And I knew it was something bad and it filled me with dread. But it didn't do anything, not then, it was just there, staring in at me.

'Then one night it got right up against the glass. And I was running madly around my house but I couldn't get away from it. Everywhere I ran it was there, peering in at me. And I know this sounds just like a nightmare, but it was more than that, because even when I woke up I could sense it still there, just behind the darkness, waiting. Some nights I'd even glimpse it, just like you did, just for a second. It never leaves me. It's here now.

'But then I had my great plan.' She looked away. 'You see, I'd read about spirits and how they haunt people because they can't fit in anywhere, they're lost. And then Angie mentioned this trip to Abbotts Hill and I thought, that's it, I'll go there and maybe give this spirit a place to go, a place to belong. I know it sounds crazy now, but I was desperate and this seemed like my last chance to be rid of it. And I felt it belonged there. So I went to Abbotts Hill and inside my head I was saying, "Leave me now, this is your new home. You are lost no more."

'And when I got home that night I really thought it had gone. I was free at last. But somehow I couldn't quite believe it. I wondered if this was another trick. And then I dreamt I saw it again – on the night you stayed over, actually. Only this time it had got inside the house. It was there in the

109

room with me. I saw this dark thing reach out for me and I couldn't move. It was like, when you're standing on a platform and a train rushes past and you think you're going to be swept away by the force – it was like that. It rushed through me and I was shaking and screaming and I couldn't wake up. I couldn't get away from it. I . . .' She faltered and for a moment terror flooded her face. 'I couldn't move, Rich. That's what really scared me. And next time it will destroy me. That's why it won't leave. For it knows, in the end I will have to sleep.

'And it's so cunning. Like it let me think I lost it at Abbotts Hill. But all that happened was you picked it up too. Believe me, Rich, that's the last thing I meant to happen.'

'It's not your fault,' I said.

'Yes it is,' she cried.

'No, not at all. This spirit can just jump into people's heads whenever it wants. I saw it, or rather I imagined it, before I saw you. In a way, I've always sensed it.'

'But it's me that it wants, me that it's calling up. It will never let me go. But you can still get away.' She gave an uneasy laugh. 'That's why I could never go out with you. I mean, Louise, what a great girlfriend she is, she even slips you a dark spirit. There's nothing I can do about it. But you can still escape. For after your exorcism, it's left you alone, hasn't it?'

I thought of the voice on the phone last night. And what I'd seen outside my house today. But that wasn't the dark spirit. That was a boy – Ben? Well, maybe. I didn't know for certain. But something was still haunting me.

I didn't tell Louise this, though. Right now, I just wanted to protect her, help her. So instead, I said, 'Yes, the dark spirit has left me alone.'

She got up. 'Thanks, Rich, you've been great. But now you're free . . .' She stretched out a hand to me, then whispered, 'Goodbye.'

'What are you talking about?' I said. Then I took her in my arms. She was shaking.

'No, Rich, you can't help me. It will never let me go and when I fall asleep . . . Oh Rich, where did it come from?'

'I don't know,' I said, slowly.

'I just know it's reaching out for me and I can't stop it.' She closed her eyes. 'And I feel so strange, as if I'm about to pass out. I can't stay awake much longer.' She opened her eyes again. 'Please go,' she said.

'As you once said to me, "Don't you dare even think about it." I'm not going anywhere. I'm going to stay here and help you.' We sat down on the couch together. She looked so white and tired I ached to help her. Then I had an idea.

'When I was younger and had nightmares, my nan used to say, think of good things, all the things you like. Fill your head with them.'

Louise settled herself on my shoulder, and asked, 'So did you?'

'Yes.'

'And did it work?'

'It did, actually.'

'Tell me what you thought about.'

111

'I can't remember now, that was years ago.'

'Yes you can, please.'

'All right. I'd often think of the sea, and imagine myself walking along the beach and there'd be a clear blue sky, not one single cloud and it'd be the first day of the holidays. But then I also love it when it snows in winter. So next I'd picture myself out walking when the snow's falling and I was just getting lost in it. And the sun would be shining and there wouldn't be any wind.'

I paused.

'Don't stop,' murmured Louise.

'Oh, I can babble like this for hours.' I said. 'What else do I like: white shirts and dark sunglasses – that's smart, cafés where you can sit outside . . .' I chatted on and on, while all the time darting glances at Louise, until I saw she was asleep. I watched her, curled up and still, her face resting on her hand. I always hated watching people asleep. It made me feel alone, abandoned. That's why I often used to wake people up – sometimes they were none too happy about it.

And now Louise was far away. It was only me now. I hated that thought so much I wanted to wake her up instantly. But I knew I couldn't. She needed to sleep. But where was she? Was she walking along the beach I'd described? Maybe she was out in the snow. Or perhaps she was re-visiting some special memory of her own. She could be anywhere just provided she'd sneaked past – it.

The dark shape I saw in Ben's room. Could that really have jumped out of Louise's head and into mine?

112

I had to think. But I couldn't, because all of a sudden I just felt this terrible heaviness in my whole body. My eyes closed and I hadn't the strength to open them again. I was rushing away too . . . further and further.

I jumped awake. I think I'd been dreaming. But I couldn't be sure. I gazed down at Louise, still curled up against my shoulder, her hair brushing my neck. She gave a little sigh. I put my arm around her.

It felt as if I'd been asleep for hours. I wondered what time it was. I squinted around me. And then I knew. The dead hour; that's what this time was, when there were more dead roaming the earth than there were blades of grass.

Then, as soft as a shadow, Louise was on her feet. I watched her start moving towards the door. 'Get away from me,' she whispered. I ran in front of her. I had to wake her up. Yet, I didn't want to jolt her awake.

'Louise, Louise,' my voice cut through the terrible darkness.

'No,' she gasped, then suddenly she opened her eyes. 'Where . . . where?' she cried, as consciousness came crashing back.

'It's all right . . . you're safe.'

She clung on to me. 'It was there, waiting, just like I thought it would be. Nothing can stop it. And if you hadn't woken me up . . .'

Suddenly I started in horror; it was as if someone had turned on a torch behind me and in one blinding flash I saw . . . My heart gave a terrible thud, which seemed to fill my head. I let out a sob, which turned into a yell.

113

'Rich, what is it?' gasped Louise.

I said, slowly, 'It's my nan, she's dead. I know she is.'

Tears escaped down my face; I brushed them away furiously. Then, dazedly, I stumbled to my feet. 'I should do something. I should see my family.' I hovered uncertainly, gazing at Louise's deathly pale face.

'We'll both go,' she said softly. 'I'll just leave a note for my mum.'

She went upstairs while I stumbled outside. The street lights were in full bloom, casting an orange-coloured glow over everything. It didn't seem dark at all, just very quiet and still. Sometimes I'd go for walks with Danny at this time. Other times I'd be on my own, dancing along the road to whatever was on my headphones. All the terrors in my room were banished; out here I owned the world.

Louise appeared and we drove away along the empty roads. An occasional lorry rattled noisily past, that was all. Every so often Louise would smile reassuringly at me, otherwise she seemed far away.

We reached Nan's road. All the bungalows were in darkness – and probably had been since ten o'clock – except one. This was ablaze with light, a cruel, horrible light. I looked away, I couldn't go in. Not yet. Instead, I started babbling to Louise. When I was little I'd come to see Nan with my parents and, for a special treat, they'd let me ring the bell. There'd be a little pause while Nan got to the door, then she'd say, 'Ooh,' and give me a hug, followed by either, 'But you should do your coat right up' or, 'I expect you're hungry, aren't you?' I looked again at Nan's house. The light was blinding now. Louise reached across and squeezed my hand.

'I'll wait here for you,' she said.

'But I want you . . .'

'I'll only be in the way. Just leave a tape on, will you, any tape.'

I knew why she'd said that and felt suddenly anxious for her. 'Look, come in, you don't want to sit out here on your own.'

'Yes I do, the music will stop me . . . I'll be fine. Honestly.'

I got out of the car. Now, everything seemed totally unreal and confused. I walked up the drive in a kind of trance. I rang the doorbell. Nan will open the door, of course, just like she always does. Come on, Nan. Don't let me down. But it was my mum who opened the door. And right away, I saw that tonight was just as unreal for her. She turned bleary red eyes towards me.

Don't say the words, Mum. Never say them. I know, all right.

But she did say them. 'Your nan's gone, Richard. She passed peacefully away at two o'clock this morning.' But the words slipped past me.

I went inside. Dad was in the hallway with Aunt Marion and Uncle David. 'I was out of the room when we lost your nan,' said Mum. 'I'd been with her all night but then I left and . . .'

Aunt Marion touched Mum lightly on the shoulder, and said, 'Richard, your nan had been sleeping when she suddenly raised herself, stretched out her hands and gave the loveliest smile you ever saw, then she fell back, gave a little sigh – and was gone.'

'I'd just left for a moment,' repeated Mum, guiltily.

'It was a very peaceful end,' said Aunt Marion.

Now a woman I recognised as the nurse was smiling dimly and saying, 'I've set up some tea for us in the lounge.'

Already, it was the lounge, not Nan's lounge. Nothing in here belonged to Nan any more. And soon, I thought, this house will be totally plundered. At once, I wanted to spike everything with razor blades.

'I've just been looking at some of her photographs,' said the nurse. 'She travelled a lot in her younger days, didn't she?'

'Oh yes,' said Aunt Marion. 'Loved to travel; travel and people, they were her passions. She was always a people person.' She smiled fondly.

But I thought of Nan living here on her own, waiting for a visit or a phone call. Often she'd ring up and say, 'You didn't just call, did you, only the phone stopped ringing before I could get to it . . .' and my parents and I would smile at the transparency of her little lie.

I remembered, with a sudden ache, how rarely I visited her. I had a car, for goodness sake. Yet I never popped round to see her. No one did, much. And now we were all sitting round, having a nice cosy reminisce over a cup of tea.

'Tea, Richard?' asked Aunt Marion.

'No, thanks.' I couldn't even sit down. I couldn't do anything. Nan had been ill for ages, but still when it happened, I wasn't prepared for it at all. Before, I'd just blocked it out. Now . . . now I was crying inside, crying with rage and pain and despair – and guilt. Terrible guilt.

Nan, I'm sorry. I was a rubbish grandson. I took everything you had to offer and then when you became sick and frail, I disappeared. And now it was too late.

I thought again of how I'd seen Nan's death. It was like a great flash of lightning inside my head. But in that instant I knew. How did I know? In a way, I suppose, I'd foretold it a few days before when I saw the Spirit of Death.

Now I was being totally absurd. Poor Nan, you wouldn't like any of this stuff about the dark spirit, would you? I don't like it either. I just want you back so that I can whisper 'Sorry' in your ear. Nan, if I say 'sorry' now, will you hear me?

I stood up. I couldn't sit around reminiscing. I had to do something. That's when I asked, 'Can I see my nan?'

Suddenly, everyone was staring at me oddly. I tried to explain. 'I wanted to say, "Goodbye".'

I'd heard people say that in films. I think everyone else had too, for my mum, after glancing at my dad, said, 'Just for a moment then.' She got up and walked with me to Nan's bedroom. 'Do you want me to . . .?'

I shook my head.

'All right,' said my mum slowly. Then she added, 'She's sleeping peacefully now.'

I opened the door. It was a while since I'd been in here. When I was little I'd snuggle down in bed beside my nan and eat all her boiled sweets. Then I felt so safe and secure.

Now I stood at the bottom of the bed, afraid of being repelled, of seeing something horrible. The curtains were drawn, but her little bedside lamp was on. The room felt intensely still. I didn't think I could move. But I did. Slowly, I crept forward.

And there was my nan. Her skin was slightly yellow and looked very taut and tight. Her mouth was slightly open but her eyes were closed; those eyes that had always seemed filled with so much light.

I knelt down and touched her forehead; already she was beginning to chill.

Now I wanted to talk to her, just like people do in films. Only there was no point. There was no point in even saying, 'Goodbye', because Nan wasn't here. Whatever it was that had been my nan, had gone away.

Where are you, Nan? They say you're sleeping peacefully. But really you're dreaming, aren't you? And now you've found such a wonderful dream you'd rather be there than wake up. So you're not coming back, are you? Not ever. But you are somewhere, aren't you, Nan?

You are somewhere.

CHAPTER 11

'I KNOW WHY BEN'S WAITING FOR US'

I walked back into the kitchen. Mum, Dad, Uncle
David, Aunt Marion, and the nurse, were all sitting
round the table, talking in low voices about people
they had to contact. Mum was writing out a list.
On the table was a pot of tea, a plate of bread and
butter and some cake. I exchanged tiny, glazed
smiles with my mum. And Aunt Marion said, 'She
looks very peaceful, doesn't she?'

People always say that. Just like they always
say, 'lovely funeral'. I remember at my grandad's
funeral, that's all anyone said – that and how he
was buried near this field of horses, which everyone thought was wonderful as he liked horses.

But now they were putting on those solemn
voices – which always sounded so false to me – and
dusting off the old clichés for my nan. No wonder
I couldn't breathe in here. I had to get away. So I
mumbled a few words to Mum and then fled to
my car and Louise.

She was huddled in the corner, her eyes
closed. I leant over her. And at once she started,
guiltily.

'I just closed my eyes for a second and then I started drifting off . . . if you hadn't woken me . . .' She stared at me in a kind of daze. Then it was as if she saw me for the first time.

'Your nan,' she whispered. 'She . . .'

I didn't need to say anything, we just held on to each other for ages. Finally, I said, 'Is it okay if I drive around for a bit?'

'Yes, sure,' she murmured.

As I drove off I said, 'I usually end up driving around in the country at night for some obscure reason. It's pretty eerie actually, especially when you stare into your rear-view mirror and you can't see anything behind you, nothing at all. It's as if you haven't been anywhere and aren't going anywhere either. Your whole perspective changes. Yet, somehow, I like that feeling, probably because I know I'm safe cruising along in my own little world of light.'

Louise broke in. 'I like that idea. It makes me feel as if we're in a kind of spaceship, exploring a strange, dark planet.' Then she added, 'I also like going nowhere.'

'It's the only place to go,' I said.

Outside it was really windy and I could feel the wind pushing against the car, making it sway from side to side. 'Any second now we're going to take off,' I cried. I pulled into the side of the road and wound the window down a little. At once I could hear the wind rustling through the trees, making a swishing sound that made me think of the sea.

'If we're where I think we are,' I said, 'there's nothing but fields around here. I came up here on my bike with some friends once. We hauled up half a ton of picnic stuff and they all hated the place, said there was nothing here. But that's why I like it. It's the kind of view you see from trains sometimes, mile after mile of open countryside flashing past. Nothing man-made at all – except for the telephone wires.'

'What I'd like to do,' said Louise, 'is buy up all these fields, just so they can never rip them up and turn them into some bloody shopping centre.'

'Oh, they will,' I said, gloomily. 'One day Woolworths will be right here.' I pointed into the darkness. We were silent for a moment.

'How are you feeling?' I asked.

'All right . . . a bit more awake, anyway. How about you?'

'Yeah. Better. I couldn't have stayed in that house another minute, you know. Out here I can think.' I smiled.

'What?'

'I was just remembering something about Nan.'

'What's that?'

I shook my head. 'You must be sick of me going on about Nan.'

'No, I'd like to hear. Honestly.'

'It was one Easter, when I was about eight or nine. I made her an Easter card and on the front I drew this revoltingly fluffy yellow chicken and inside I wrote: "You're no spring chicken but I do love you." Well my mum thought the card was rude and didn't want me to send it, but I did – and Nan just laughed and laughed. That was one thing about Nan, she never let you down. I let her down, though.'

'No, you didn't,' said Louise.

We were silent again, then I said, 'I don't see the point of funerals. I mean, you don't have people standing around in suits being formal when you're born.'

'You have christenings,' said Louise.

I brushed this aside. 'No, I don't want a funeral. I don't even want to be buried. I want my body to be used for something useful, like the skeleton they have in science lessons. Now I'd love to be that.'

Louise started to laugh. 'Would you really?'

'Definitely. I don't need my body and it'd be put to good use. We had a skeleton at our school and it amused us, we liked it. We stuck a cigarette in its mouth once. We got chucked out of the class for that. But still, you might say the skeleton was young again, rebelling with the gang.'

'And it was dead and still smoking,' said Louise, 'which can't be bad.'

'Exactly, that skeleton was having fun. And look at Yorick from *Hamlet*. He may be only a skull but he's still centre-stage, isn't he; he's even in adverts.' I stopped for a moment, Louise still half-smiling at me, then I said, 'I saw Nan tonight.'

'You saw her?'

'I know it sounds weird but it was all right . . . not scary or anything. Just this strange stillness and a really strong feeling that Nan wasn't there any more.' I stopped. A few seconds ago I'd made Louise laugh. Now in the corners of her eyes I saw terror. 'I'm sorry,' I said. 'I didn't mean to . . .'

'No, no,' she whispered. 'It's only, when we lost Ben, I wanted to see him to say "Goodbye" but his bed had this terrible screen all around it and I couldn't move.' She started to shiver. I closed the window at once, but she went on shivering. 'I didn't want to see him like that. That's why I didn't go,' she cried.

'There's no reason why you should have done.'

'It wasn't true that I didn't care,' said Louise. 'It's just if it was true, if Ben really had gone, nothing made sense, or ever would again. How could Ben, a healthy six-year-old, just die? There must be some mistake. Ben hadn't gone. And sometimes I'd wake up in the morning and, for a moment, feel he was there, looking at me, wondering why I wasn't talking to him. Does that sound crazy?'

'Not at all,' I said.

'Once or twice I'd even hear him running about, bouncing his ball, and I'd shoot up in bed.' She let out a sigh. 'I haven't dared tell anyone this before, because Mum can't bear to talk about him. She even packed all the pictures of him away. Once or twice I've heard her in this room and I know she's been crying. And his room – well, you've seen it – it's just like a shrine. But she can never speak about him. I mean, my mum's great and yet she and I spend all our time pretending and that frightens me. Especially as I can't help feeling that Ben isn't far away. But that's not possible, is it?'

'I don't know,' I said slowly.

'No, he's gone. Everything else is just imagination. It's only, I'd love to think there was a chance . . .' She was looking at me, almost pleadingly. I knew I had to say something.

'Harry said, sometimes it takes a while for children to realise they are on the spirit side. They stay in their old homes and can't understand why we're ignoring . . .'

Louise broke in. 'You've been talking to Harry, the medium that Danny knows?'

'Only briefly,' I said.

'But you said he was rubbish.'

'No, he's all right. I don't agree with everything he says, but . . .'

'Why did you see him though?' asked Louise.

I hesitated.

She was looking directly at me now.

I hesitated again. Then I thought, Louise has sensed Ben in the house too. She was already halfway to what I was going to tell her.

'I think I'm being haunted,' I began.

'But I explained that,' said Louise.

'No, it isn't just the dark spirit I've seen,' I said. 'You remember the night of the massive thunderstorm? Well, after I'd dropped you home, I got back and the answer-phone kept switching on. I think it was because there were all these little power cuts. Anyway, I went downstairs and the phone rang, just the once. I picked the phone up and I heard this voice saying, "Let me in, let me in." It was a young boy's voice.'

Louise let out a gasp.

'That was all the voice said, then the line went dead. That's why I went to see that medium. He said there had been a number of examples of spirits somehow communicating by phone. Anyway, afterwards, I dropped Danny home and then I was just walking into my house when I saw someone standing in my doorway – except he wasn't so much standing as floating there. It was a boy, about six years old.'

'Ben,' whispered Louise.

'It looked a bit like him. I couldn't be sure though, and there was something disturbing about him. So I said these words Harry told me to use and he disappeared instantly.'

'But he can come back, can't he?' said Louise.

'I don't know,' I replied. 'Maybe he has moved on . . . Harry said that's what all spirits have to do in the end.'

'But he can't, yet,' cried Louise. 'Poor Ben must think I turned my back on him.' She was staring into the air and she wasn't so much talking to me as thinking aloud. But then her eyes found me. 'Maybe our minds are so close, you've not only picked up the dark spirit but Ben, too. Do you think he's got a message for me?' She didn't wait for me to answer. 'I must see him, so he knows that . . . poor little Ben. Where is he? At your house?'

'That's where he was.'

'He'll still be there,' cried Louise. 'He must be. We'd better hurry, Rich.'

I said, 'Okay, then. The only trouble is, I always get lost down these country roads.'

I was trying to sound easy and light-hearted. But then I looked across at Louise. She was sitting very still now. I sensed her excitement and tension. What was I doing to her? What if we didn't see Ben? And then I started to question what I'd seen. For it wasn't how people see spirits in films – then the spirits hang around for ages in glorious techni-colour. This was so brief, so scrappy, a snatch of a voice on the phone, a fleeting glimpse outside my house. Was I giving Louise false hope? Louise, who seemed to be swaying with tiredness now. Louise, who was so tormented, she'd created this dark force which was destroying her. Louise, whom I want to help more than anything in the world.

Outside now was so dark, it was as if someone had slammed a black velvet bag over my head. But at least I knew what lay behind the blackness.

But the other darkness. Could I see through that, too? Had I really picked up Louise's brother, signalling desperately to us? I thought again of that picture of Ben, in his room, grinning cheekily in his baseball cap. The figure I'd glimpsed sitting on my bed and outside my house, twisting about in such a strange way. Was that really Ben too? It was as if I were trying to do a jigsaw, only too many of the pieces were missing to form any kind of picture.

Louise stumbled out of my car. 'Come on, Rich. I know Ben's waiting for us.'

As we walked up my drive I remembered again the strange figure I'd seen suspended in the air. I really wished I hadn't panicked, hadn't chanted those words at him. Still, he couldn't be far away, could he?

We went inside. I asked, 'Would you like a coffee or . . . ?'

'No thanks. I just want to see Ben.'

Suddenly, her vulnerability was almost impossible to bear. For a moment, I turned away. She was expecting too much from me. I couldn't just summon up her brother for her. I didn't even know if it was her brother. Not really.

My stomach turned over. I was sick with nerves. But I just said, 'Maybe if we try my bedroom first.'

Louise was up the stairs at once. Inside my bedroom I went to put on a light.

'No, don't switch on the lights,' said Louise. She sat down on my white canvas chair.

'Don't expect any miracles,' I said.

Louise didn't seem to hear. 'Do you sense him here?' she said.

'Not yet,' I said. 'Usually the first sign is, it starts to get cold.' I stopped. I didn't know what I was talking about. I was a hopeless amateur where all this was concerned.

But Louise was rushing on. 'That time when I was here before and it went cold, we thought it was the dark spirit but maybe, instead, it was just poor little Ben struggling to get through.'

'But what about the dark figure I saw in the mirror?' I said.

'Oh, yes, I was forgetting that,' replied Louise, quietly.

The dark figure I'd created – or rather Louise and I had. What about Ben? Had I just imagined him, too? Or had I, as Harry believed, opened myself up to one lost spirit? Would I ever really know?

We sat in silence for a few minutes while around us the air was suddenly very still. It was as if it had frozen into something and we were waiting for it to crack open.

For some reason, I kept staring down at my bedclothes. Were they moving? Could I detect the slightest movement? Any second now, would some invisible hand start tugging at the sheets?

I started moving to the side of the bed. I didn't know how strong Ben was. Then I said, over and over to myself, 'Yes, do it Ben, lift those bedclothes, give us a sign.'

I strained my eyes. The bedclothes certainly looked as if they were about to take flight. But then I wondered if it was just like those times when you stare so hard at a painting, the figures seem to start moving. It was all an illusion really: imagination run riot.

Then I heard Louise cry, 'Listen.'

'What?' I whispered.

'Don't you hear it?' she said.

I listened again. 'No.'

'There's a tapping noise.'

I stiffened. 'That's what I heard before,' I said.

'I know. So you must hear it now,' she cried. 'It's very faint.'

But I couldn't hear a thing.

'Rich, open the window,' cried Louise. 'It's Ben tapping to be let in. I know it is.'

At once, I had a picture of me opening the window and some unknown force rushing in. Something we couldn't control. I hesitated.

'It must be Ben, please,' cried Louise. Then she got up herself.

'It's all right, I'll do it,' I said. The window swung open and cold air gushed in.

Louise walked over to the window like someone in a trance. 'Ben.' She had her arms outstretched. 'Ben, please,' she whispered. 'I've missed you so much. Come back. Please come back.' She was standing right by the window now, the cold air rushing at her. 'Ben,' she whispered, so softly I could hardly hear. 'Ben.' But now, her words were like a lost echo.

She slowly sat down again. 'Will you leave the window open?'

'Sure,' I said.

'I did hear something. I know I did.' Then she added, in a voice choked with tiredness and frustration, 'He must hear me now.' Her pain was making me tremble. But then I thought, what were we doing up here? We wanted to touch the other world. The world my nan entered tonight. My nan, who earlier today was so frail, you could break her with one finger: somewhere was she young Nan again? But how young? And did she stay that age? I didn't know. No one did, not really, did they?

Suddenly, everything seemed so unknowable. It was like last year when I was on holiday and I went for a walk along the seashore at night. And there was the sea roaring away, so vast and endless, it made me feel pitiful. So then I start shouting at the sea, which was totally stupid. But it was all I could do. Not that it made any difference, of course. And that was all I was doing now, shouting into the unknown. No wonder all that came back were echoes of me.

'You can close the window now,' said Louise, wearily.

'We can leave it a bit . . .'

'No, close it,' said Louise. 'I don't even know if I heard the tapping noise now.' Then she whispered, 'I nearly had him back, anyway.' And I thought bitterly, why did I have to tell her about Ben, pumping her full of false hope. It was almost as if he had died again.

She went on, 'But it wouldn't have been any good really, for I want him to come back properly. I want to play football in the park with him again. I want to make him laugh. I want to put my arms around him. I want him to stay. But he won't. He can't do that, can he?'

'No,' I said, gently.

'He's been gone over a year now,' cried Louise, 'and I still miss him so much. I know I should move on, but I can't. I can't let him go.'

She got up and switched the lights on. 'You've been great, you really have. Would you mind taking me home now? I just can't stay awake any longer. I'm completely wrecked.'

'But what about . . .?'

She shook her head. 'Suddenly, I just don't care.' There was no colour in her face at all now. Not any.

I got up too. 'Ben could still be here,' I said.

'Yes, yes.' Her voice wavered. And then her eyes caught sight of Ben's pad on my chest of drawers. She picked it up.

'Have it back,' I said. She hesitated. 'Go on, it belongs to you. I only really borrowed it.'

'Would you mind if I did? It's just, I bought him this and the last time I saw him, he was so ill and yet, he was still asking for this pad. It was the last thing he . . . Thanks, Rich.'

We went outside. It was starting to get light. Louise just collapsed into the car. I wanted to help her so badly, and yet, in a few minutes she'd be far away, facing what she most feared. I felt totally useless.

I had to say something. 'If it's any help,' I said, finally, 'and it probably isn't, once I had this nightmare which kept returning: the nightmare was that I was on top of this skyscraper, which started tilting backwards. The nightmare always ended with me falling, but I never hit the ground. I just had this sensation of falling. And I'd always wake up with this horrible feeling that I couldn't move, couldn't breathe. Every night it happened. Until, one night, just before I fell asleep, I started picturing a different ending to the dream. This time I had a parachute and I landed safely and smoothly in a green field.'

I stopped. I'd reached Louise's house. She had her eyes closed and I wasn't sure she'd even heard me. But then she opened her eyes and asked, 'And did it work?'

'Yes, I had a great time floating about in the sky.

131

I was quite disappointed when I woke up. Never had that dream again.'

'So you think I could do that, imagine myself defeating the dark shape?'

'Just remember what you said to me: you created it, so you can destroy it.' But even as I said that, doubts crept in. All at once I wanted her to stay awake. I was afraid for her.

She leaned forward, picked up Ben's pad, then kissed me lightly on the lips. 'Thanks for coming round,' she said.

'I'm sorry we didn't see Ben,' I replied.

She looked away and stared into the pale, white morning. 'If you do see . . .'

'I promise,' I said.

She was opening the car door when I blurted out, 'I wish I could go with you.'

She looked across at me. 'Perhaps you will,' she said.

I hugged her, hard. Then I had to watch her walk up the drive. She turned round and waved, just like she had the first time I brought her home.

I drove off, but all the way home I was following Louise. I pictured her walking up the stairs and checking on her mum. Then – yes – she'd stumble downstairs and make her mum a drink. And then she would fall into bed. She'd be closing her eyes about now. And, almost at once, she would start slipping away . . . any second now, she'd be asleep.

A tremor ran through my body. I longed to shout out a warning to her, stop her. But it was too late. She'd crossed over . . . she was gone.

I went inside my house. Moments later the phone rang. It was my mum. We talked about Nan. Tears started to form. In the night I'd believed Nan was somewhere else. But now it was as if I had to tell it to myself all over again. It hurt, badly. Then Mum and Dad told me they'd be home later today. I was quite shocked at how pleased I was about that.

I was about to crawl upstairs when Danny and Angie rang. They were full of questions. I just told them Louise hadn't been sleeping too well lately but she was fast asleep now. Yet even as I said that, I had to swallow back a horrible feeling of dread.

And after I put the phone down I started picturing Louise sleeping on for hours, if not days, while I stood on guard over her, anxiously waiting for her to return. Then the doctor told me that she'd probably never wake up. She was trapped in a nightmare that wouldn't release her. The dark spirit was claiming her, taking her away from me, for ever.

'Louise,' I started to call out to her. 'You created the dark spirit, you can destroy it. Just come back, Louise, wherever you are.'

BY LOUISE

My house is dead. That's why it is so cold.
I'm standing in the lounge. I always end up here.
Nothing ever changes, except this time . . .

I walk up to the lounge window. No, it's not
outside. I know where it is.

An icy sweat bursts over my forehead.

I can't see it yet but I know it's here in this room
with me.

I cry softly to myself. This time it will destroy
me. Then, from somewhere deep inside me, comes
Rich's voice, 'Fight back. Fight back.'

I want to fight back, Rich. I really do. But
look how the room is growing darker, making me
cough. And there is this terrible dark fog sticking
to me. I try and shake it off but it only clings on
to me all the tighter.

And then I see it, looming over me: it is
everywhere now. There is no escape. I can't lose
it, not ever. I feel as if I'm about to pass out. I
close my eyes. And then up comes Rich's voice.
'You created the dark spirit so you can destroy
it.' Over and over he says it, until finally I gaze

through the smothering darkness and see it, darker than the thickest blackness, except for its eyes. Its purple eyes. I gaze at them in astonishment. I never noticed its eyes before. They look bizarre. Purple eyes. Then I remember Rich said something about giving the monster purple eyes. And of course, it is our creation.

I stare into those dark, glowing eyes.

'I want you to go. GO!'

Nothing happens. For a moment I hesitate. Maybe it is stronger than me. But then I brush aside this thought and cry, 'It's no good. I know what you are. And I want you to dissolve away. NOW!'

All at once the darkness does start to clear, just a little.

'Go on,' I say.

I move forward and it's then my hand touches something, my fingers slide over it. Then I draw back uneasily. I've just touched a gravestone. I can read the inscription. *Here lies the body of Ben Ray*.

I stare at it disbelievingly. Then I let out a cry, a terrible cry which tears me apart. 'Ben,' I yell.

And it's then I hear it, way off somewhere, a voice calling my name, high and far away. It can't be. It's a trick. Only, there is the voice again, much closer now. A voice I know so well. I whisper his name to myself, still unable to believe it – and then I shout his name as loud as I can.

'Ben!!!'

I shout it so loudly the darkness seems to shake.

'Ben,' I shout again. And now . . . now I can see right through the darkness to . . . Ben's room.

I peer around me. What am I doing here? I must have fallen asleep in here. Maybe I wanted to be near Ben. Yes, that was it. Funny, I don't even remember going to sleep.

But now I'm awake again. The dark spirit couldn't hold me, not when I heard . . . My eyes fly open. There it is again. Ben's voice, calling for me. He's somewhere in this room.

I scramble off the bed, shaking with excitement. 'Ben, where are you?'

For a moment there's just silence and then I hear his voice, so near to me I catch my breath. But of course, I know where he is. It's a game we often used to play. He'll be where he always hid, in the gap between his bed and the table, waiting for me to say, 'I wonder where Ben is?'

I say the words now. And then I hear a muffled giggling. What a weird game this is. He knows I know where he is. Yet still it gives him pleasure. So I continue the ritual. 'I guess Ben must have gone out.' And that was always when . . . when . . . a voice cries, 'Louise, I'm here,' and there he is, grinning away at me, saying, 'I've been waiting for you to find me. It's taken you ages this time.'

I help him out of his hiding place. Then I kiss and hug him, laughing and shouting and holding on to his arm tightly, so he won't vanish away again. 'I'll never let you out of my sight now,' I cry.

He moves away from me, shrugging his shoulders. 'You're funny,' he says, 'making so much fuss. I've been here all the time trying to get you to notice me. You got me so mad sometimes. I even tried telling your boyfriend,' he adds, flashing one of his mischievous smiles.

'He's not exactly my boyfriend.'

'Yes, he is,' cries Ben. 'I've seen you.' Then he starts dancing around me. 'Louise has got a boyfriend, Louise has got a boyfriend!'

'You haven't changed,' I say. 'Still as annoying as ever.'

'I want to play a game,' says Ben. 'You play as well.'

'Yes, all right.'

He looks amazed. 'You're not actually going to play a game with me, are you?'

'I often play games with you.'

'You're always promising to play with me, after dinner, after I've done my homework.' Ben starts bouncing his ball around me. 'After I've washed my hair, after I've gone into town . . .'

I interrupt. 'What about the time I played ball with you and you smashed that Japanese plate and guess who got the blame?'

Ben starts to laugh, and then we are both laughing. 'Let me go and get Mum,' I said.

Ben considered this. 'No, let her sleep. She's not been well. I've been watching her.'

'Have you?' I whisper. 'But she will be all right?'

'Oh, yeah.' At once he stops bouncing his ball. Ben will do that, play some game madly for a few minutes and then just abandon it.

'Where's my chemistry set?' he asks.

'In the top drawer, exactly where you left it. Do you want to play with it?'

'Yes . . . No.' Ben pauses, as if he's trying to remember something. 'I want to tell you something, show you.'

'Show me what?' I ask.

He pauses again then says, 'I'm going to draw you a picture.' He goes over to his desk and immediately checks the felt tips in his mug.

'It's okay,' I say. 'They're all there.' He picks up his pad.

'What are you going to draw now?'

He taps his nose and grins. He never liked you looking over his shoulder when he was drawing, so instead I sit on his bed, watching him, wonderingly. I still can't believe he's here. I feel quite dizzy with happiness.

'Your boyfriend,' says Ben unexpectedly. 'He's all right. He's sound.'

'Sound.' I smile at the way he takes up words he's heard older boys use. But I reply, softly, 'Yes, he's sound all right.'

'Do you think you'll marry him?' he asks.

'Only you can ask silly questions like that.' Then I add, 'I wish he were here now, to see you.'

Ben looks up. 'Actually, I think I scared him.' He looks suddenly wistful. 'I scare everyone. I don't know why. You can see it now, Louise.'

I go over to the desk, leaning down beside him. He explains, 'There's this tunnel, see, and just beyond the tunnel there's this amazing castle and it's made up of so many colours, you can't take your eyes off it. I want to live in that castle.'

'It's really good,' I say. 'Where did you get the idea?'

'It's what I saw,' replies Ben. 'And I want to see it again, but I want you to see it too. Will you, Louise?'

'Yes, sure. But where is it?'

'It's not far away and that castle is so amazing.' He flashes me one of his grins. 'Come on, my rocking sis.'

He puts his hand out to me. I seize hold of it. 'We'll have to leave a note for Mum. How are we going to get there?'

He laughs. 'But it's really near. It's only through there,' and at once, he's scrambling through the gap between his table and the bed. 'Come on, sis,' he calls.

I lean down. 'But I can't follow you down there. Ben . . . Ben, wait.'

Then I hear his voice again, much further away now. 'Look, there it is, right ahead of us.'

'But I can't see anything,' I cry, desperately. 'Ben, come back!' There's no reply.

'Ben! Ben!'

And then I just catch his voice. 'I'll be back for you, sis. I promise . . . promise.'

'Ben, wait,' I scream. This time there's no reply, just a huge silence. I weep tears of frustration. Ben was here with me, why did I let him go? But I couldn't stop him. If only I could have followed him. I stare downwards. There must be a way through that gap.

I kneel down. 'Ben,' I cry, not expecting any reply. But I do hear a voice, from high above me.

It's Rich's voice. He sounds urgent, too. I get up. Then I hear Rich's voice again. It's pulling me upwards.

All at once I find myself floating higher and higher. But how can I be doing this? It's impossible. Unless . . and then I land in my bedroom again.

I sit up in bed. And I watch the rain drumming against the window, while thinking to myself, that wasn't just a dream. It really was Ben that I saw. He was there, walking around, being himself. He even drew me a picture, a beautiful picture.

I reach out for Ben's pad. I open it at the page of me playing the guitar. MY ROKEING SIS. And I feel such a yearning for him again. All I have left of him now are these pictures. Dreamily I pore over them.

There is his really good picture of that train he saw and there is . . . there is a long tunnel and right at the end of the tunnel is a castle with shining yellow turrets and above it, splashes of every colour you can think of . . . I gaze at it in wonderment. Any moment now it will dissolve away again. I even run my hand over the picture to make sure it is real.

But where has it come from? Has it suddenly just appeared? Or was it always here, waiting for me to see it, to really see it? Then Ben's words come rushing back: 'I want to tell you something, show you.'

I stare right into the picture, then I clasp it to me. Ben's last gift to me.

Ben, you've done it, you've broken through. Now at last I see. I know. Don't worry, I'll tell Mum, Rich, everyone. And you – you are free at last.

Ben, I'll never forget you. Not even when I'm an old, old lady. Actually, that's perhaps when I'll see you best. For even though you'll have gone so far ahead, I know you'll come back for me, just like you promised.

My bedroom door opens a crack. Mum, in her dressing gown, is standing there.

'Oh, you are awake,' she declares.

'Yes, I've just woken up,' I say. 'How are you feeling?'

'Much better . . . I think you're the one who needs to rest now.'

'Mum. I've just had a dream; I saw Ben.'

She starts. We haven't said Ben's name aloud for such a long time. The word pierces her. She stares in front of her, then whispers, 'Ben, my poor little Ben. Sometimes at night I think I catch sight of him, just for a moment, and I run forward, but it always turns out to be someone else . . . one of the pupils at school, a neighbour's son, never Ben . . . I'm glad you found him.'

For a moment her eyes lock into mine. Then she says, 'I really must sort his room out, one day. Some child would . . .' She breaks off. 'It's a shame, all those toys and games lying idle.'

'I'll help you,' I say.

She half-smiles. 'Yes, we'll do it together, soon. But anyway, I'm forgetting, you've got a visitor downstairs: Richard. He's been pacing around the kitchen, asking if you're awake yet. Do you want him to come up?'

'Oh yes,' I cry so eagerly Mum catches my happiness – and for a moment, her eyes are alight, too.

'I'd better get him,' she says, 'before he explodes with impatience.'

And half a second later, there is Rich, standing in the doorway.

He looks awkward, nervous. I smile up at him. Now he is standing by my bed. He stares at me incredulously. 'The dark spirit . . . you . . .'

I reach out to him. And he is in my arms as I whisper, 'Rich, we won.'

A Selected List of Fiction from Mammoth

☐	7497 0343 1	**The Stone Menagerie**	Anne Fine	£2.99
☐	7497 1793 9	**Ten Hours to Live**	Pete Johnson	£3.50
☐	7497 0281 8	**The Homeward Bounders**	Diana Wynne Jones	£3.50
☐	7497 1061 6	**A Little Love Song**	Michelle Magorian	£3.99
☐	7497 1482 4	**Writing in Martian**	Andrew Matthews	£2.99
☐	7497 0323 7	**Silver**	Norma Fox Mazer	£3.50
☐	7497 0325 3	**The Girl of his Dreams**	Harry Mazer	£2.99
☐	7497 1699 1	**You Just Don't Listen!**	Sam McBratney	£2.99
☐	7497 1849 8	**Prices**	David McRobbie	£3.50
☐	7497 0558 2	**Frankie's Story**	Catherine Sefton	£2.99
☐	7497 1291 0	**The Spirit House**	William Sleator	£2.99
☐	7497 1777 7	**The Island and the Ring**	Laura C Stevenson	£3.99
☐	7497 1685 1	**The Boy in the Bubble**	Ian Strachan	£3.50
☐	7497 0009 2	**Secret Diary of Adrian Mole**	Sue Townsend	£3.50
☐	7497 1015 2	**Come Lucky April**	Jean Ure	£3.50
☐	7497 1824 2	**Do Over**	Rachel Vail	£3.50
☐	7497 0147 1	**A Walk on the Wild Side**	Robert Westall	£3.50